Larry Reed
Enjoy
Joey Crowley
12-21

A SHIP IN THE DESERT

JAY CROWLEY

Sweet Dreams Books

ISBN-10: 1530235723

ISBN-13: 978-1530235728

ASIN: B01DI4MG7E

Email: jaycrowleybooks@gmail.com

Like me on Facebook: Jay Crowley-Sweet Dreams Books

For updates on new stories and more information on the author or books, visit www.sweetdreamsbooks.com

If you enjoy the book, please leave a review on Amazon, our Facebook page, or both, as it is helpful to the author. Thank you.

DEDICATION

I would like to dedicate this story to my friends and family who have supported me in my writing endeavor. Also, out of the kindness of their hearts, they corrected my grammar and hopefully caught all my punctuation errors. I especially want to thank Ann and Josie, the Grammar and Punctuation Queens. Thanks also to my husband, who loves to tear my stories apart. I used some of his military expertise in this story. A big thanks also to my editor, Alan Seeger of Five59 Publishing.

I hope you enjoy the story as much as I enjoyed writing it. Nevada has a lot of interesting stories to tell. It's so much fun to weave them into my tales. Northern Nevada is so versatile — from beautiful Lake Tahoe to the wide open desert, which has a beauty of its own. Nevada is 85 percent under the control of the Bureau of Land Management, the National Forest Service, the U.S. Military and Native American reservations. Based on that alone, there are lots of stories to tell, ranging from before the Civil War to the present day.

In researching this story, I learned a lot about post-traumatic stress disorder (PTSD). We need to do so much more for our veterans who suffer from this condition as well as their families. God Bless them.

Thank you, one and all.

Jay

TABLE OF CONTENTS

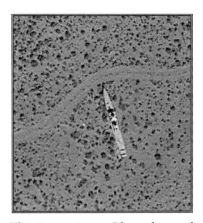

This image is not Photoshopped.

Tuesday evening...

The intruders went upstairs, methodically moving from room to room. They were wearing night vision goggles, making it easy for them to see within the darkened house. When they went into the master bedroom and saw the sleeping bodies on the bed, they shot them. There was little noise, thanks to the suppressors on their weapons.

They walked over to the bed and pulled back the covers. One of the men said, "Shit... these are *pillows!*" They started looking around to see where Brad and Angela, the occupants of the house, might be. One looked under the bed, another in the bathroom and the third looked in the closet. Then they heard the sirens.

"Shit! I thought you cut the alarm!" shouted one of the men. With the cops coming, the men started pulling out of the house. The whole maneuver was completed in military style, in and out fast.

Chapter 1

Ever since Brad Benson was a child, his Uncle Jim had talked about a ship in the desert outside Hawthorne, Nevada. Uncle Jim told him how the U.S. Navy practiced dry bombing the cement ship throughout World War II. He went on to mention how the Navy had been slow to recognize the value of air power that could be used against naval vessels. The Navy was appalled when, in 1921, General William "Billy" Mitchell used planes to bomb and sink naval ships.

Gen. Mitchell himself said, "The day has passed when armies on the ground or navies on the sea can be the arbiter of a nation's destiny in war. The main power of defense and the power of initiative against an enemy have passed to the air." According to the history books, Jim explained, Gen. Mitchell had pointed out the vulnerability of Pearl Harbor, Hawaii to air attacks. However, the military and political leadership of the day disagreed with Mitchell and ignored his warnings. Sadly, Mitchell's foresight came to fruition some twenty years later, when the Japanese attacked Pearl Harbor on December 7, 1941, later immortalized by President Franklin Delano Roosevelt as "A day which will live in infamy."

More than 300 Japanese fighter planes, bombers, and torpedo planes attacked the Hawaiian base on that day. All eight U.S. Navy battleships were in port; four were sunk and four were severely damaged. Two, the *Arizona* and the *Oklahoma,* were total losses, with more than 1,500 dead on those two ships alone.

The *West Virginia* and the *California* were sunk as well, but were repaired and returned to service later in the war. The *Nevada* was hit by six bombs and a torpedo and was beached, but returned to service less than a year later. The *Pennsylvania,* which had been in drydock, was damaged but remained in service. The *Tennessee* and the *Maryland* were each hit by two bombs but were both back at sea three months later.

Three cruisers and three destroyers were also in port, and suffered various levels of damage. Thankfully, the three Pacific Fleet aircraft carriers (Enterprise, Lexington, and Saratoga) were out at sea at the time of the attack.

Despite all this, we still had a Navy that could fight, much to the surprise of the Japanese, and win the war. However, according to Jim, the era of the battleship was over, and the aircraft carriers had come into their own. Brad loved to listen to his Uncle tell these stories.

There is little or no data regarding the target ship and how it arrived in the Nevada desert. It's assumed that after the Pearl Harbor attack, the military hauled the 120-foot cement ship into the desert for training. At the time, it had to have been quite a feat and at a significant cost. Of course, the price didn't mean much to the military. Therefore, even if the ship was built where it sits, hauling in all the supplies had to have been a massive and costly endeavor.

Jim said that the ship was created for the training of pilots; that this battleship-shaped cement ship was just that, a mock-up target for high altitude bomber training which assisted the United States in winning the war. This type of training taught the pilots where and how to hit the enemy ships. They were trained to go in quickly, strike, sink the enemy ship, and leave.

Jim was proud of his service in the war. He had enlisted just before he turned seventeen, having lied about his age. It was by pure luck that he became a pilot; flying seemed to come naturally to him.

The Army also built simulated towns in the Nevada desert. They placed lifelike dummies in the buildings to see what the effects of artillery shelling and bombs would have on people and property. This training was intense for its time. Uncle Jim also talked about an underground Navy submarine base located under the Nevada desert, and how the Navy used Walker Lake to practice wartime submarine maneuvers. Brad never knew if that was true, as Uncle Jim would often tell tall tales.

Is there a possibility that the Navy does operate submarines from Ford Ord, California, using an underground sea tunnel which extends underneath the Sierra Nevada mountain range to the Naval Undersea Warfare Center outside of Hawthorne? Even today there is a sign saying Naval Undersea Warfare Center and a gate shack with guards, so who knows? Perhaps Uncle Jim was right.

According to Jim, the military base had set up all this training in the middle of the desert so it would not be observed by the outside community or hostile nations. To protect their security, they built the base hundreds of miles from any city. However, with the growth of the State of Nevada, a major highway now goes right through a portion of this area. The ammunition dump is quite visible from the road.

Nonetheless, Brad always wanted to see the ship himself. He could only imagine the planes practicing dry bombing on the cement vessel. Because of his Uncle Jim and his stories, Brad had grown up wanting to be an Air Force pilot. However, when he joined the Air

Force a few years later, they had other plans for him, as you will see. For years, Brad and Jim talked about going to see the ship in the desert, but life kept getting in the way.

It was finally decided that when Brad got home from Iraq for good, they would make the hike. However, while Brad was still in Iraq, Jim developed an aggressive stomach cancer and within six months, he quietly passed away. Brad could not come home for the funeral to say goodbye. It was a devastating blow to him.

Jim had been more like Brad's father rather than an uncle. Brad's father had died in a car wreck when Brad was only ten, and Jim helped to fill the void. Brad's mother, Mary, was a little woman with bad lungs, perpetually in ill health. Therefore, Uncle Jim was Brad's savior.

After the death of her husband, Mary never went anywhere. She was, to a great extent, bed-ridden. Brad was the oldest of the siblings by two years; his twin sisters, Beth and Barbara, were eight when their father died, so Brad became the man of the house. Life changed for all of them after their father's death. Brad and his sisters were thankful for Uncle Jim and Aunt Ruby as well. Ruby took the girls under her wing, and taught the twins how to cook and sew. She was also a staunch supporter of the three children in their schoolwork and school activities. They all made the honor roll at school. Brad played football and the girls played softball. Ruby and Jim were a blessing.

Jim was half Paiute on his mother's side and proud to be so. Brad's dad had never talked about his Native American roots, but because of his heritage, Jim taught Brad to appreciate Mother Earth and feel blessed that he was part Paiute. They went camping, fishing, and hunting together quite frequently, while Ruby and the girls stayed at home. Jim taught Brad how to shoot and about life. When Brad got older, they drank beer and played checkers. Jim loved to cheat at the game, which made it fun. Uncle Jim was a happy-go-lucky sort of man with a heart of gold. Together with his loving wife Ruby, they were great role models for the Benson kids.

Ruby and the girls cooked all the fish and game that Brad and Jim brought home. Mary participated in some of the fun as well, but she was too ill to do much. When Brad was twenty-one, Mary passed away as well, leaving him to oversee his sisters. Since Brad and his girlfriend Angela had just gotten married, the twins decided to live with Uncle Jim and Aunt Ruby, but Brad helped support them, since they both were going to beauty school. They were a very close family and helped each other when in need. Sometimes the girls, who were now 19, would come and visit as Angela was about their age and loved her sister-in-laws too.

As the hot summer was drawing to a close and the weather was starting to cool, Brad, Angela, and their dog Macks were planning a hiking trip to Hawthorne. Brad was sorry his Uncle Jim was not around to go on the trip they'd always planned. Going to see the cement ship was an adventure they'd planned for years, and now it was only two weeks away.

Brad still hadn't gotten over the loss of his uncle and missed him a lot. He loved talking to his uncle and missed his stories. They say time heals all wounds, but Brad still hurt for the loss of his Uncle Jim.

Brad wasn't sure just where the ship was supposed to be located. However, with today's technology and Google Maps, he soon found the vessel outside the Hawthorne area and printed out a picture. He saw that a small road went past the bow of the ship. The road, however, was old and overgrown with sage brush in spots; most likely it was built by the military years ago when they used the land.

By the early 1960's, the major part of the military had left the Babbitt Army base, located a few miles outside Hawthorne. The USAF Strategic Air Command (SAC) radar station was established within the remains of the Babbitt base, and was there from 1961-1985. The Department of Defense (DOD) transferred the SAC headquarters to the U.S. Navy base in Fallon until it closed in 1994. Fallon is a "Top Gun" Naval base and still quite active today. In fact, the movie "Top Gun" was filmed there. The base puts on a great air show every year.

People always laugh when they hear the U.S. Navy has a base in the Nevada desert. Nevertheless, people like to watch them perform flying maneuvers over the desert outside of Fallon as well as the dry bombing runs. The Navy used to let the community hold drag races on their runways. That went on for years until private citizens built their own track outside of town. The military and the Fallon community have always worked together.

The land around the ship still belongs to the DOD, but they have deactivated the base and placed the property under the control of the Bureau of Land Management (BLM). Anyone can go into the area, but he or she must obtain a permit, which is good for ten days. The permit is needed, as it is still considered military land.

The area where the ship is located cannot be accessed by motor vehicles; you can only hike. The walk to the ship is around twenty miles from Highway 95, which is the main highway running to and from Hawthorne.

Brad had read a lot about the history of Hawthorne. The railroad created and named the town after a Carson City lumberman. There is a lake in the center of the valley, called Walker Lake, but currently, it is in despair due to four years of drought. Around the lake to the north is the Paiute Indian reservation located at Schurz. The Paiute are peaceful now, but in the early days of settlement, they sometimes raided the town and travelers in the area. Brad wanted to visit Schurz and talk to some of the tribal members, since he was part Colorado Paiute.

Today, Hawthorne is kept alive mainly by the DOD ammunition storage facility, and it is the primary employer in the area. The facility was built for the DOD and the Army during World War II. The town itself has been aligned with the military since before World War II and they are very patriotic. However, due to cutbacks in military forces in the 1990s, the base at Babbitt was deactivated and has since largely been torn down. Nonetheless, the ammunition facility is still active and operates under a civilian contractor on behalf of the DOD, since the facility is on military lands. Army personnel still reside in Hawthorne and oversee the general operations of the ammunition facility.

When Angela was very young, her parents, Sue and Bill Brown, loved to go up to Virginia City. It is a classic old western town with great bars and shops. It had a significant role in mining history and Nevada becoming a state. There was so much to see and do up there that she and her parents often spent the entire day browsing the shops or visiting friends. The world found out about Virginia City due to the 1960s television show "Bonanza." Tourists worldwide came to visit and to relive the old wild west, with its gunfights and stagecoach rides. Back then, the tourists all wanted to meet the Cartwrights. Even today, they still come to Virginia City to see the wild west.

The Browns often went to Virginia City, and as they visited with friends, at night they watched the ammunition facility burn off excess ammunition in Hawthorne; it was like the Aurora Borealis. Back then, Nevada had a very small population — less than one million folks. Hawthorne was the only major town for miles in that area, so there wasn't any light pollution to block the sights. The lights from Hawthorne would be visible for hundreds of miles. Locals used to say Virginia City had a thousand mile view at its 6800 foot elevation, and that you could see the A-bomb tests in Mercury. That wasn't actually true, but you certainly could see the 'burning off' of the ammunition from Hawthorne a couple hundred miles away.

However, when the military pulled out in the 90's, the ammunition burns stopped and the Aurora Borealis went away.

Brad and Angela were having fun planning their trip, purchasing the supplies they would need and deciding what sights to see. Brad had received all the proper hiking permits for Angela, Macks and himself. He even bought a handheld GPS system, a pair of binoculars, a new 35mm camera and some MRE's (**M**eals **R**eady to **E**at), just in case. Brad thought there might be water in the area but wasn't sure if it was drinkable, because of the drought, so he bought a bottle of water purification tablets, just in case. Each of their backpacks contained plenty of food, a water camel, four bottles of water and a couple of canteens. They also packed a three-man pup tent and two sleeping bags.

They figured it would take a little over a day to get to the ship and the same to return. For the trip, each of them took a week's vacation from work. This amount of time would allow them nine days to see the ship and enjoy other things of interest in the area, like Schurz.

Realizing the Hawthorne area could be quite warm in the summertime, Brad and Angela decided to wait until late summer to make the hike. It would be the longest excursion they had ever attempted, so they considered not taking Macks along. In the end, however, they decided that he was, after all, part of the family, and they did not want to board him out, so he would go too. They would keep a close eye on him and make sure he did not get bitten by a rattlesnake or become dehydrated. Also, they would only try to walk ten miles each day; so he should be fine.

Brad worked as a Civil Engineer for the State of Nevada, and Angela was a full-time secretary for an insurance firm. Both were looking forward to a change of pace from their normal lives. Angela was also attending nursing school part-time at night. She liked that profession better than being a secretary. She planned to graduate the following January, after which she would go to work at the local hospital.

They both found hiking to be relaxing and it gave them a break from their daily routine of work and school. They were both anticipating the trip, and Brad thought of it as a last goodbye to his uncle. They knew the trip could be hazardous, but both of them were excellent marksmen and would carry handguns, mainly for snakes or the occasional aggressive coyote. They also were trained survivalists and loved to camp, so they were prepared — or so they thought.

Brad, an avid gun enthusiast, had a concealed weapons permit. He had been in Iraq with the Air Force, so guns were second nature to him; Angela, not so much. When Brad was in the service, he had been a "Red Hat" with the Air Force. Their motto was "First There," reaffirming the Combat Controller's commitment to the undertaking of the most dangerous missions. The Red Hats went behind enemy lines, leading the way for other forces to follow. Brad went into those combat zones, making way for the Marines and the Army.

The Red Hats' mission in Iraq was as Air Force Special Operations Command's Combat Controllers. These airmen were assigned to special tactics flights. Brad was trained in special operations forces. He had become certified by the Federal Aviation Administration as an air traffic controller. His mission was to deploy, undetected, into combat and hostile environments to conduct special reconnaissance and establish assault zones or airfields. Brad was trained to do this while simultaneously conducting air traffic control, fire support, and/or command control and communications (C3) plus forward air control. He did whatever was needed to secure the target.

He was deployed with air and ground forces in support of the direct action of whatever was needed, such as counterterrorism, foreign internal defense, or humanitarian assistance, and combat search and rescue. As a Combat Controller, he was trained to operate all-terrain vehicles, amphibious vehicles, weapons and demolitions in pursuit of mission objectives, which could also include obstacle destruction. He was trained to do it all.

Brad served as a Red Hat in Iraq for two tours of ten months each. He served in the Air Force for a little over four years until he was honorably discharged with post-traumatic stress disorder, better known as PTSD.

So what is PTSD? When an individual feels as if he or she is in danger, it's natural to feel afraid. According to medical sites, "This fear triggers many split-second changes in the body to prepare yourself to defend against the danger or to avoid it. This 'fight-or-flight' response is a healthy reaction meant to protect a person from harm. However, for a person with PTSD, their reaction is changed or damaged. People who have PTSD may feel stressed or frightened even when they are no longer in danger." Brad did not trust anyone except his wife. Its a horrible feeling of being paranoid all the time.

Brad had bouts of anger and lost control over little things. Before he went for counseling, he drank too much and would, at times, become very aggressive. To keep the peace, Brad and Angela stayed home, as he felt safe there. Angela would work with him and he would calm down if she was there. However, she was not always able to be home, and then all hell would break loose. He had been escorted home several times by the local police for bar fighting. Everyone in their small town knew Brad, so the police gave him a break, and he was not arrested.

Brad often had severe headaches and nightmares. Life was hard on both of them. Finally, after much encouraging from Angela, he went for twelve weeks of counseling offered by the local hospital. The Veteran's Administration hospital in Reno didn't offer much help for a vet with his condition. The long-term counseling he received helped them both to survive and saved their marriage. The counseling consisted of training on how to meditate and let things go. There was also a new procedure that was being used at military bases, which started at Fort Carson in Colorado Springs. Some of the Lakota people had built a sweat lodge *(Inipi* in Lakota) to help veterans with PTSD. It worked so well it was being tried in other areas, so during the last five weeks of Brad's counseling, he went to a Lakota sweat lodge twice a week in Fallon on the Navy base. During the sweats, he finally found peace and centered himself.

The sweat lodge was built out of blankets and was nearly airtight. The medicine man would make a fire in the morning and place rocks in the flames. By afternoon, the rocks were red hot. Then the medicine man would haul them into the center of the sweat lodge, put the stones in a pit, and pour water on them. Brad and several other vets suffering from PTSD entered the lodge with the Lakota medicine man. Some of the vets were not Natives, but simply people in need. The medicine man then passed around the pipe filled with traditional herbs, and they all smoked. The first seven stones were placed in the center of the lodge and the door was closed tightly, and the first round of the Inipi began. Everyone sat in a circle around the hot stones. The number of stones increased as the ceremony went on. By the time it got to round three, Brad felt like he was inhaling fire and the sweat was pouring out of him.

It had gotten so hot in the sweat lodge that the only way he could breathe was through a wet towel. The medicine man sang prayers in the Lakota language and splashed water over the pile of hot stones. The water evaporated instantly and new waves of heat overwhelmed all of Brad's senses. Some of the people around Brad were singing, crying or chanting, but he could not see them; the darkness of the lodge blotted out everything. The smoke from the burning sage and the steam from the stones made the air thick and heavy with vapors. Brad wasn't sure he could last through it, but he knew he had to. It took all the endurance he could muster for him to last all three rounds, but for Brad, the sweat was a godsend; it helped remove the negativity in his life and ground him. He was at peace, at least for a while. He trusted the medicine man and looked forward to going to the sweat lodge and finding that peace.

Another centering technique Brad learned to use to overcome his feelings of paranoia was grounding. Stop. Breathe. What is overstimulating you? Is the feeling rational? These were things he would ask himself. One of the things Brad had problems with was being in a crowd. When in Iraq, crowds were a bad thing, because today's modern warfare doesn't have enemies in uniform. He began to imagine that all the people around him were hiding the enemy. When he got home, he wanted to isolate himself because of it. However, Angela wouldn't allow that. He hated crowds. But in reality, not everyone in a crowd is the enemy. Not everyone is out to get him. Not everyone wants to do him harm. Stop. Breathe. Look around, not scanning, just looking. Brad learned to ask himself, "Is it rational to assume everyone is the enemy?" The answer is no. Not everyone wanted to harm him. Breathe a little more, then relax.

Brad knew this sounded a bit simple. The way you think really does influence the way you feel. It takes time and practice, but it can be done. Brad would learn to control this condition over time, according to the shrinks. Brad also learned to realize that he was his own master and this condition would not control his life. He would overcome it.

Thank goodness, Brad was never abusive to Angela, or it would have been the end of their relationship right then and there. Some veterans who suffer from PTSD become abusive to their loved ones. In fact, one of Brad's fellow Red Hats had killed his wife and a police officer in a domestic situation. Living with PTSD is awful for everyone involved, mainly because people look at the person with PTSD and see nothing wrong. It's not a visible issue like a broken leg. Brad was told that part of his healing was to talk about the disease like an alcoholic, so people could help him if he started slipping.

It was a blessing for Brad that he trusted Angela. She learned to calm him down and help him get control of his life. However, when she was out of his sight, he would wonder what she was doing. Was she planning on leaving him? His mind would run wild. The paranoia was driving him crazy. He didn't know what he would do if he lost her.

Angela loved him dearly and she had the patience of a saint. She knew this was not Brad's doing; it was the condition. Between her and the counseling, he was coming to grips with the condition. He meditated and took deep breaths to calm himself. It worked most of the time. However, he still couldn't handle a lot of stress or crowds. So he tried to avoid pressure, and that worked for a while, but as we all know, life is stressful. He had been learning to cope, working on it for a year or more. He might get the condition under control and he might not; either way, it would take time.

According to medical journals, PTSD usually develops after a terrifying ordeal that involves physical harm or the threat of physical harm to an individual. With Brad, he had seen too much carnage from the war during his two tours in Iraq. Even after seeing women and children being killed, he could still cope. But on the last part of his second tour, it was different; it was worse. During that tour, Brad developed the PTSD from an event that happened to his flight. Being the Master Sergeant, he was responsible for these men.

It was a typical day in Iraq, whatever that was considered to be. The flight was on a routine mission. They were putting down runway markers for an airfield they were building when they were ambushed by insurgents. The enemy had sighted in on his squad without him or the men knowing it and started shooting at them without warning. The insurgents fired rocket-propelled grenades (RPG), as well as both light and heavy automatic weapons. Brad's squad did not have the same firepower that the insurgents were using. They were only armed with light automatic weapons. In addition, the insurgents were too close to his men for Brad to call in air support for fear of being hit by friendly fire. As the battle progressed, three of his five-man squad were killed. Two of his men were blown up by RPGs. Finally, after what seemed like an eternity of fighting, the surviving member of the squad was far enough from their attackers for Brad to call for air strikes to neutralize the enemy. Afterwards he was able to carry the last remaining wounded airman to a safe spot.

While the air strikes were going on, the pararescue team (PJ) came in and evacuated them out of harm's way to receive medical care. When the enemy had been killed or dispersed, the PJ's removed the dead from both sides. After the area was safe again, another group of controllers came and completed the mission. Brad felt he was a failure; he had let his men down.

Both he and the fellow surviving airman, Bryon Hackmore, were severely wounded. Over time, they both recovered physically, but suffered from PTSD. Both airmen were awarded the Purple Heart for their injuries as well as the Bronze Star for valor. However, there wasn't a day that went by when Brad didn't think about the firefight and what he could have done to prevent it. He blamed himself for the incident, thinking he could have done more and been quicker in killing the enemy and saving his men. He continued to have nightmares about the incident in which he heard the sounds of the rocket launchers, the smell of the gunpowder and the screams of his men.

Some of what Brad remembered was in his head, and it did not necessarily happen the way he remembered it. The Air Force investigated the incident and it was decided that there was nothing Brad could have done differently to prevent the attack and protect his men.

However, Brad always thought there was more he could have done to keep them safe. He feared the day the terrorists would come to the United States, and he believed it would be soon. Most of the time that fear bordered on paranoia; that was a part of the PTSD.

Before he went off to war, Brad and Angela were high school sweethearts. They both went to Carson schools, and that is where they met. Angela was sixteen and first met Brad at a football game. Brad was a couple of years older and had graduated from high school in June. He was an eighteen-year-old freshman at the University of

Nevada and was visiting his old buddies on the football team, since he had been a teammate for several years. They saw each other, and it was love at first sight.

He had remembered seeing her when he was a senior, but he was too shy to talk to her. That all changed that night. They became the best of friends and soon fell in love.

They got married when he was not quite twenty-one and she had just turned eighteen. He was a junior in college, and she had just graduated from high school.

Money was tight, trying to work and go to school. In addition, Brad was helping with his sisters' education, so he decided he would join the military to get the GI Bill, which would help him finish college.

Brad enlisted in the Air Force, as he wanted to fly like Uncle Jim. However, Brad was a good shot and he didn't fear anything, thanks to his Uncle. Those qualities, plus, being a strapping, six-foot, well-built young man, made him a good candidate for the "Red Hats." He was proud that the Air Force had selected him as a Red Hat, but in his heart, he wanted to fly, not build runways.

After almost two years of harsh training and watching eighty-five percent of his classmates get washed out of the program, Brad graduated as a Master Sergeant. Angela stayed home, worked and waited. Time went by and she knew that he would soon be home for good. The plan was that he would only serve four years in the Air Force. However, that was extended to almost six years. Knowing that the time would go by quickly was what kept her going; she missed him so much. To save money, she stayed with her folks while he was gone. Angela was blessed that she was not alone during this period of time. So between her job, going to nursing school part-time, and helping Aunt Rudy with Brad's sisters' education, Angela's life was busy and the time went by fast. Brad's sisters were about the same age as Angela, and they had gone to school together. Both girls were now going to beauty school. Beth was engaged, and the wedding was set for September. Barbara was dating, but hadn't found a serious relationship yet.

When Brad came home on leave, He was able to see Beth get married; in fact, he gave her away at her wedding. He didn't talk much about what he did in the military. Angela and the family had never heard much about the Red Hats, so they never asked what he did for the Air Force. Angela was also naïve about what Brad was doing in Iraq; she never felt he was in any real danger. So when Angela received the call from the Chaplain that Brad had been wounded, it upset her and the whole family. It scared her. She thought she was going to lose him.

Worse yet, he was sent to the Wiesbaden Army Hospital in Germany, and she was in Nevada. Angela didn't have the money to make the trip to Germany, and if she had, she would have had to stay there for months until he was sent stateside. So she stayed at home and called the hospital every day. Most of the time she talked to the nurses who cared for him.

Then came the day she was finally able to speak to him. "Brad, honey, I've missed you so much. How are you doing?"

"Better, now that I get to talk to you. How are things at home?"

"Everyone's doing fine. Beth is expecting in October. You're going to be an uncle!"

They talked for quite a while, and her stress eased up a bit. Angela thought Brad would be okay in time. Plus now she could talk to him every other day. The doctors said that he needed all the rest he could get. She could still call every day and talk to a nurse. However, after thinking it over, she decided to call every other day and talk with Brad.

Brad was in the hospital in Germany for months; it seemed like years for them. Finally, the Air Force transferred him stateside. Because Brad had been severely wounded, they placed him in an Air Force Medical Center in Colorado, closer to home. It was still a distance, but a lot closer than Germany. He was in that hospital for several more months. However, at least Angela could fly out and visit him; she made the trip every two weeks. She had gotten a second job as a waitress to help pay for the airfare and the trip expenses. Angela was stretched between the two jobs and school and visiting Brad. *But*, she thought, *this won't be forever.*

The doctors had removed the shrapnel and many of the bullets. However, they could not remove one of the bullets from Brad's chest, for fear of doing more damage to his lungs. The bullet was causing severe infection, so the wound wouldn't heal. They finally placed a Wound-Vac on the opening, and he had to wear it for months. Nevertheless, with the support of family and friends and the power of prayer, he finally pulled through, physically restored. They were so lucky; he was healthy and young. He had all his limbs; he would be okay in time. By the time he came home, he was an uncle to baby James Lewis Carter, named after his Uncle Jim.

The other surviving airman, Bryon, wasn't so lucky. He had lost his left hand and his right leg. However, he was able to get fitted with both a hand and leg prosthesis, and with therapy, would be on the road to recovery. He also suffered from severe PTSD, he didn't have the family support that Brad had. In fact, Bryon had no family. While he was in the hospital in Germany, his mother and father, who were visiting him at the hospital, were shot outside a restaurant by a suspected group of terrorists. Life was not good for Bryon, he did not have anyone like Uncle Jim and Aunt Ruby.

Angela knew they could make it through anything as long as she and Brad were together. When she learned that he was suffering from severe bouts of PTSD, she was not sure what it was and had heard horror stories. So she went online and researched the condition. At first she was not sure she could handle it. Nonetheless, she knew she loved Brad and knew what a wonderful guy he was. She was determined that they would work together to help him get over this hurdle in his life. Angela was an eternal optimist — always seeing the glass half full.

When they knew they needed help with his condition, Brad enrolled in the twelve weeks of counseling as an outpatient. The counselor also taught Angela how to watch for the stress signs, what to expect and how to handle it. They were both strong; she was sure they would overcome and control the PTSD in time, with lots of patience and love.

When Brad first got out of the service, he went back to college on his GI Bill to finish his engineering degree. He took eighteen credits a semester and went to summer school. It took him less than a year to complete his degree.

Brad was now almost 28, and Angela was 25, so they had a full life ahead of them. Then there was Macks, their rescue dog. They got him when he was about four months old from a puppy mill. Macks was solid black, except for a white diamond on his forehead. He was a Lab-Pit mix male with lots of energy, and at times, he could be a handful. However, he was their joy. Since they had no children, Macks was their kid. Basically, they were your average, healthy young couple, full of life and adventure.

With Brad going to counseling, and not drinking in excess any more, life got somewhat back to normal. Both sisters were now married, and Barbara was expecting. With the extra money he had saved from no longer supporting his sisters and the promotion received after he finished his degree, they decided to buy a house. They bought a three-bedroom, two-bath house in Washoe Valley, which is between Carson City and Reno. It was a rural area, but still close to the two cities. The ranch-style house had a wrap-around porch in front of the house, allowing them to see the view from any angle. There was also a small deck in the back of the house. The house was situated on three acres of land on the west side of the Sierra Nevada mountains. It also contained a big basement and a food cellar. The basement was built into the hillside, so the temperature never changed; it would always stay around fifty degrees. However, it was heated by the floor furnace. The laundry room was also in the basement.

The two-thousand square foot home had no close neighbors and had an awesome view of Washoe Lake and the Washoe Valley. The front room window looked right over the lake. With its beautiful back deck and fenced-in yard that ran up the side of the mountain, Macks loved it, as it was C-scape. Brad had a barbecue grill on the back deck. The front porch was protected from the wind, and they often ate out there during the warm weather.

The winds in Washoe Valley can get quite fierce all year long. When the winds are blowing, big trucks and motor homes are forbidden to drive through the valley; they must go around on the rim. However, on occasion during a wind storm, someone in a high profile vehicle will ignore the rules and try to drive through the valley, and they often end up being tipped over. Locals know the risk and don't try, but people from out of the area often think they can make it. Sometimes they do, sometimes they don't.

The Washoe Valley surrounds Washoe Lake. U.S. Route 580 goes right through the center of the valley, heading north and south. This area was an agricultural region for many years. People raised horses and cattle as well. Basically, it's a bowl between two mountain ranges, with a lake in the center. The valley is about five miles long and perhaps fifteen miles wide. Living high up on the west side of the valley gave them a magnificent view of the entire valley as well as the lake.

Brad and Angela loved their home. Brad had built his own sweat lodge in the backyard for him and Angela, which they also shared with other people in need. Angela had planted a small garden, as she loved to work in the dirt. There were mature apple and peach trees that came with the property, so she also canned fruit in the fall. They also had pine and elm trees on the property, which offered some additional privacy from the neighbors down the road. Someday Angela thought they would build a barn and have a cow and some chickens, maybe in the spring. That would depend on how much money they could save. Both of them preferred to pay cash for everything and not use credit cards. Angela had watched her parents use credit cards; she had seen the effects of charging too much. Now her parents were in debt. She thought, *We have a house payment, and that is enough for us right now.*

They had no children at this point in their lives, but they were working on it. They would have liked to have two or three kids, but Angela felt time was running out for them, so they might only have one child. Besides, they now had a nephew and a niece to play with and spoil. Angela and Brad watched the kids now and then, to give their parents a break. Aunt Ruby helped as well, but she was now in her seventies, and it was hard for her to take care of little ones.

Both Angela and Brad had grown up in Nevada, though Brad originally came from Colorado. His folks moved to Carson City when he was six. Angela, on the other hand, was born in Carson City. They liked the rural life of Northern Nevada; there was so much to see and do, and in fact, they had never lived anywhere else.

Brad and Angela loved skiing, and Mount Rose was just a few miles from the house. Heavenly Ski Resort and Kirkwood Ski Lodge were only a little farther away. Brad had taken up snowboarding, but it wasn't Angela's cup of tea. She liked downhill slalom or cross country skiing. In the winter, if there was enough powder, they would go skiing once a week.

Their house was perfect for what Brad had in mind. He broke through the outside basement wall and continued to expand into the side of the mountain. Brad constructed an 18x20 foot room that no one would know was there. He didn't apply for a building permit, so it wouldn't show up on any blueprints. Brad dug out the room with a small backhoe he'd rented. He took the dirt out through an escape tunnel he'd created. The twenty-yard tunnel ran from the room to a knoll he had built down the side of the mountain. Brad then planted native brushes on the knoll, so it was well hidden. Then he poured cement walls inside for the new room and part of the tunnel. He also created ventilation shafts which were hidden on the outside of the room, just in case they were needed. With his paranoia, everything was always "just in case."

Brad was quite a craftsman; he also created a wall and a steel door, both sixteen inches thick, on the inside basement side by the stairway. The door to his secret room was not noticeable, as it looked like part of the basement wall. He'd set up a push button to release the opening of the door. Only he and Angela knew where to find it. With the door shut, no one would suspect that there was a secret room on the other side of the basement wall. The escape exit, should someone find it, also had a thick steel door at the outside entrance. Brad also had another door at the opening, coming from the tunnel into the secret room, just in case. So basically, the exit tunnel had double doors. He had crafted the doors himself. His secret place was a fortress; he had planned it that way. Brad had learned to build these types of places in the military. He modified some things, hoping no one could find the doors or the ventilation pipes.

The inside of the room was stocked with everything they would need to survive. There was food, water, guns, ammo, a gas-powered generator, a hand-cranked generator, an oxygen concentrator, a satellite radio, and a satellite telephone. Brad also placed cameras at various points around the property so he could observe any activity on the property or inside the house from this room. Some of the cameras outside were visible, such as the animal cameras, while others were hidden. He even ran trip wire alarms around the escape tunnel outside the door in the soil, just in case someone was prowling around. They would be warned inside the room.

On his desk were a desktop computer and printer. His big investment was a twenty-five hundred watt inverter with wet cell batteries. This was set up to run the electronics. If and when he used the inverter, he could recharge it with either of the generators. He knew he was paranoid, but he couldn't help it. Angela knew about the room, since she had helped him build it. However, that was about it; she referred to it as his man cave. She understood his PTSD, and if this room made Brad feel safe, Angela did not complain. She was not, however, aware of all the equipment he'd purchased or she would have told his counselor. Brad kept telling himself it was okay that she didn't know about everything. What was in the room was important. It might be of use someday, you never knew. Just in case.

Brad's fears might have been illogical, but because of his military training and the PTSD, this room was his haven, and it made him feel safe. If terrorists attacked, or everything went to hell, he knew Angela and Macks would be safe there. He did not want to think about losing Angela. She was his lifeline to sanity, and he loved both her and Macks very much. The thing that ate at him and scared him the most was the possibility of letting them down like he did his flight. He had to protect them. This paranoid fear was his driving force.

Chapter 2

The trip had been planned for Saturday, September 12th. Since it was after Labor Day weekend, and school had started, they hoped they would have the area by the ship to themselves. They planned to arrive at the vessel by Sunday afternoon, spend some time there, and then head back on Tuesday or Wednesday. Brad had told their families of their plans since they would not have cell service on the way to the ship. If something were to happen, God forbid, someone would come looking for them. They felt they had everything covered for the trip, but like everything in life, things don't always go the way they're planned.

While planning and getting into shape for the trip, they hiked around Spooner Lake State Park. This is on the way to Lake Tahoe, off Highway 50, at the top of Spooner Summit. It's a beautiful yet rugged five-mile walk. They thought these hikes would only help them for the long hike to the ship. They attempted to take this hike every other weekend throughout the summer. Spooner Lake was fairly close to where they lived, so it was always a fun day for them to go walking, then have dinner at the South Shore of Lake Tahoe afterward.

Macks loved this hike, and chasing the geese along the way. He knew he would be yelled at, but it was fun anyway. There were always lots of people on the trails. Some would be hiking or riding mountain bikes, and others on horses. It was a great place to hike for individuals as well as families. After a couple of miles of hiking, they stopped at their favorite spot and sat on a park bench.

"This is such a beautiful place to relax and enjoy the beauty of the lake," said Angela. "Do you want a granola bar?" she asked as she drank some water.

"Thanks, no. The water is enough. I just want to sit and enjoy the scenery. I love it up here."

"I'm so glad this is a State Park, and no one can ever build here," replied Angela as she gave Macks a jerky treat.

"I agree."

They sat in silence and listened to the geese and the sounds of lapping water; it was pure heaven. Macks seemed to think so too. He marked the trees so every dog would know he had been there.

Several hours later, as they were walking back to the car, they were relaxed and ready to eat at Chevys at the lake. This was one of their favorite restaurants for a good margarita, along with some excellent Mexican food. Macks was tired and ready to go for a ride. He loved being with his people, they did fun things. His head hung out the back window, breathing in all the wonderful smells.

Finally, the day came for their big adventure. The trip started at 8:00 AM. They drove for several hours before they arrived in the town of Hawthorne. They stopped at Maggie's restaurant, a favorite with locals, and ate a hardy breakfast. They also had a hamburger patty cooked up for Macks. Then they drove to the road that led to the ship and parked their vehicle in a large pull-off.

Macks was all excited, as he had been pent up in the car for several hours. When they stopped to let him pee on the way to Hawthorne, he didn't get to run, so he was ready now.

"Come on, Macks!" said Angela as he jumped out of the car and started running around. Macks was now two years old, but still full of energy. Even though he was a neutered male, he loved to mark his territory. There were lots of smells at the parking lot, so he proceeded to pee on all of them.

They gathered their gear from the back of their red Dodge Durango. "Let me help you with that," said Brad as he helped Angela put on her backpack. They had also attached their sleeping bags to their backpack frames. Brad had attached the pup tent to his backpack as well. Each pack weighed more than thirty pounds; mainly it was food and water. In time, that weight would decrease.

"Thanks. Do you need any help?" Angela asked.

"No, I got it." He slipped his on with ease.

Brad locked up the car, put a leash on Macks, and they headed out. Macks was pulling on the leash, enjoying all the smells and, again, peeing on everything. "Whoo Macks, calm down; we have a long walk, so save your energy and your pee," he said, laughing and smiling at Macks.

Angela smiled and laughed. "Like he understands you!" Surprisingly, Macks did quiet down.

The weather was pleasant, not too hot; in fact, it was just right. They started marching off single file. Macks leading, with Brad and Angela following. It was a worn path, so the hike went faster than they expected. They made small talk along the route, about the scenery or whatever, stopping now and then to drink some water, rest

31

and take pictures. After a little over four hours of walking, they had traveled almost 10 miles. *Wow, and it's only 3 PM*, thought Brad.

"If we keep this pace, we may be at the ship today before dark," said Brad.

"There's no rush. We need to leave enough time to set up camp and cook. Let's do another mile or less, then call it quits for today," said Angela. "Plus Macks and I are getting tired."

Brad looked at his wife, smiled and said, "Okay, that sounds good." He could see she was tired. Macks on the other hand, was still full of energy. He checked his cell. "As I suspected, still no cell service out here." They had lost signal about seven miles back. "We could hike to the creek bed, about half a mile up the road. Is that okay?"

"Sounds good. Do you think there'll be any water?" asked Angela.

"Who knows, with this drought," replied Brad.

They walked the half mile before coming to the creek. Brad had seen it on his topographical map of the area. The creek had water; it had a slight stench, plus algae on the rocks from the slow movement of the stream. Brad was surprised that there was water, since they were in a four-year drought. They found a part of the creek where the water was deeper than the rest and had a lovely, sandy beach. The water looked safe, as there were horse tracks around the stream. If they boiled the water, he figured it should be okay for them, and he had the purification tablets.

"There are wild horses out here, and this must be their watering hole. Let's set up camp here," said Brad as he dropped his backpack.

"That means other animals may water here too. You think we'll be safe?" Angela said as she looked around. "Glad we have Macks." Angela thought, *I hope I can sleep here tonight. I'm tired. I don't want coyotes coming by for a visit.*

Brad could see Angela was concerned. "Not to worry. You have me to keep you safe, babe, and we have our pistols." Brad laughed as he gave her a big hug.

Angela stuck her tongue out at him. He could read her so well. With that, she started unhooking the pup tent attached to Brad's backpack. This was the first time they had used it, but the pup tent went up easily; it was a lightweight, spring-type tent. Brad took dry food out of his pack for Macks and put it in a collapsible bowl, and poured some water into another bowl. Macks chowed down and drank some of the water. Then the two of them went off to gather wood.

Since they were by a creek, Brad felt it was safe for them to have a fire. About ten minutes later, Brad came back with an armload of dead sage for a firestarter, with Macks happily following behind him. In no time, they had hot water for coffee, food to eat and a place to sleep. Angela fed Macks some soft dog food. He was a happy camper, as he laid between them with his head on Angela's lap.

They sat around the fire with full tummies and listened to the sounds and smells of the desert. The fire crackled, with the smell of sage giving off a pleasant odor as it burned. However, the horse droppings by the creek added an unwanted fragrance. But overall, life was good.

Angela was glad for the fire; since the evening was cool, she grabbed a sweater. It was dark now, and with no light pollution, they were amazed by the number of stars and the majestic sweep of the

Milky Way curving down to the far horizon, which was invisible in the city.

"The stars are magnificent, no clouds. I am amazed that we can see so many," Angela said dreamily.

"They seem brighter here than at the house," replied Brad.

They were all alone in this vast empty expanse of desert, except for the animals that lived there. As they were talking, Macks growled and raised his head, then jumped up. Angela thought, *Shit, it's coyotes!*

"Stay, Macks," said Brad as he shone his flashlight in the direction of Macks' stare. There were three mares and a young filly about fifteen yards away from them, apparently coming in for a drink. "It's okay, Macks; it's just the horses. Good boy." With that, Macks laid his head back down. Macks liked to growl but was never a yapper. He just watched the horses, making sure they didn't hurt his people. The animals weren't afraid of them and proceeded to drink. Consequently, they stayed just far enough away that they could easily run from the humans and the furry animal.

The rest of the evening was quiet. They heard some coyotes in the far distance, but all was well. As they crawled into bed, the pup tent was crowded with the three of them. They laughed, and Angela said, " I hope Macks doesn't have gas tonight."

In the little tent, they stayed warm and safe with their brave Macks to protect them. Macks was in heaven; he was right between the two people he loved. He was smiling as he passed gas…

Chapter 3

Sunday morning came, and they had slept later than intended, but what the hoot, they were on vacation. As they lay in the tent looking at the morning, it was a start of a beautiful day; the sky was clear with no clouds. They climbed out of the tent, letting Macks do his thing while Angela stirred the coals and got the fire going again. She started heating water for coffee. Angela walked over to the creek and washed her face in the cool water, then put her long, dark hair in a ponytail. While the coffee was brewing, she and Brad rolled up their sleeping bags, attaching them to their backpacks.

The weather was crisp, but not very cold. Just the same, Angela pulled a gray jacket out of her backpack and put it on for additional warmth. One of the things she learned when you go camping or hiking in the desert was to dress in layers. If it got too warm later, she would tie the jacket around her waist, but she wanted to be prepared for now.

By the time they ate, packed up their gear and threw water and dirt on the fire to put it out, it was around 10 AM. Macks was ready to start on their trek again, so off they went. Brad told Macks to stay close to them, which he did. The high Nevada desert isn't flat like what you see on the TV shows. There can be steep mountains of shale to climb, causing a hiker to sometimes slip and slide. They were very thankful for the worn path, as it made the climbing so much easier. Brad was pleased that they were making such good time. After having hiked for just a few hours, Brad figured they would be at the ship in less than half an hour.

Angela laughed "We're making such good time because our load is lighter."

Brad laughed and said, "Yeah, it was all that food Macks ate yesterday."

Macks' ears perked up when he heard his name, and he turned and looked at them with an innocent face. They both laughed at him. They were a little over a mile away, according to the GPS, and it was not quite 1 PM. They had made excellent time.

While they were climbing what they hoped was the last mountain, they heard and then saw a chopper in the distance. It looked like a military helicopter. Instinctively, Brad told Angela to duck down beside the bushes. In fact, they all ducked by some large sagebrush and stayed crouched there. It flew over them close enough that Brad could read the chopper's tail numbers and smell the exhaust.

"Shit, it's a Blackhawk… that is a stealth-type chopper. But this area is... *was*… Army, and they do not fly… what *is* this?"

Brad was thinking, *Thank goodness we're dressed in dark clothing,* as the chopper came back by, acting like it was looking for something or someone. The helicopter then flew off in the direction of the ship. Brad didn't know why he felt as if they shouldn't let the chopper see them; he just did. Angela thought, *Come on, Brad. You're being paranoid. Will I ever get used to his PTSD? Will we ever be normal again?*

"Not sure what that was all about," said Brad. "But let's be careful, just in case."

"Well, it *is* military land. Maybe they're on some maneuver and checking out the area around the ship," explained Angela very calmly.

"Maybe, but why are they here? Let's be careful anyway." Brad was beginning to sweat. *Breathe.* It did not take much to stress him.

Just to be on the safe side, they put the leash on Macks and told him to be quiet. They continued walking the last hundred yards up the hill, and at the top they looked down, and there was the ship, sitting in the desert valley, about a hundred yards down the mountain from them. However, about that time, here came the chopper again. This time, it was carrying a large box, slung below the bottom of the 'copter. Brad thought, *That was quick. So there must be a landing field not too far from here, for him to be back so soon.* They again hid behind some large sage. Brad thought, *Thank goodness for the bushes out here.*

"What the fuck is going on? Why is it carrying a box?" mused Brad, mainly talking to himself.

The Blackhawk came in low and made a parachute drop of the box it was carrying, so that it landed lightly by the ship. The 'copter circled the area, verifying that everything looked okay, then flew off. They watched the chopper fly out of sight before they moved. As soon as they thought it was safe, they hurried down the mountain toward the ship. Approaching the area, they saw the large, sand-colored box, nearly blending in with the desert floor. It was at least six feet long by three feet wide. Brad's curiosity got the best of him as he ran to see the box and what it contained.

Angela shouted, "Don't, Brad — it could be dangerous..." but Brad ignored her and started prying it open with his hands. "Please stop, let's think about this," pleaded Angela.

Hearing her tone, Brad stopped and looked at her. "You're right. I'll bet it's a drug drop and someone will be by to pick them up. We need to get the hell out of here. We'll go back up the hill and watch what's going on from there." He stood up and took some quick pictures of the box.

Angela nodded in agreement. She was scared and didn't understand what was going on either. She just wanted away from the box. She did not know why, but she didn't feel safe. She felt as if someone was watching. They climbed back up the mountain as quickly as they could.

Brad said, "Let's get off the path a ways, just in case someone comes walking by on the walkway. There was a large sage bush over there by that big rock."

Brad used his knife to make an enclosure of bushes using one side of the big rock so that their hideaway wouldn't be noticeable from the ground or the air. Here they could hide and observe what was going on by the ship and the box and not be seen. Brad figured if anyone came looking for them, he or she would look along the path and not this far into the bushes. He laughed to himself, *sometimes my military training comes in handy.*

As she was watching him do all of this, Angela said, "I think we should go back to the car or wherever we can to get cell service and give the authorities a call." She was very anxious about the dropping of the box, though she didn't know why. All she knew was she wanted to get the heck out of there. Things didn't feel right; the hair on the back of her neck was standing up.

"By the time we go back, call the authorities and come back here again, the box will be gone. If it's drugs, we can give the authorities all the information needed for them to arrest the dealers. We can handle this; we have our guns and our survival training." Angela thought, *Brad, is in his glory, and it's scaring the shit out of me.*

Brad had to admit to himself that his adrenaline was running. Angela's face was ashen and white; she just wanted to go home. She felt that he wasn't thinking straight. *If it were a military chopper, there wouldn't be any drugs, right?* However, she didn't say anything; one thing she'd learned when he got like this was just to play along, and not to stress him any more than he already was or get him angry. They sat within the shelter and watched. It seemed like several hours passed by… nothing. In reality, it was probably only twenty or thirty minutes. Then they heard a noise that sounded like the chopper again. Brad looked across the valley and saw the Blackhawk flying along with an Army combat vehicle called a Stryker. They were coming toward the ship. "What the…? Why all the military?" Said Brad, again, mainly talking to himself.

Sure enough, it was the same chopper that flew over them before. It circled around and then flew back to the ship. Then came a desert camouflage Army Stryker. The Stryker stopped by the box. The copter flew low by the vehicle, tipped the chopper and took off into the blue-gray sky. Brad had brought binoculars, so he watched and wondered. Two people in desert camos got out of the Stryker, walked over to the box and kicked it, then they kicked it again, shouting something. Hesitantly, the lid started to open.

"Shit, it's opening from the inside, and something's getting out," explained Brad. The occupant must have said something to the people as they looked around the valley. Brad suspected they were looking for them. "Shit," said Brad.

Angela was scared to death; she thought, *I want to go home.* But they stayed put.

Brad couldn't tell what it was that got out of the box, as it was cloaked in dark clothes and it looked like it was wearing a mask or a hood that covered its face. The small figure hurriedly climbed into the Stryker, and they left in the same direction they had come from. This took all of ten minutes. They were in a hurry to leave; in fact, such a hurry, that they left the box behind.

Angela didn't know what to do or think, so she didn't move. She was frozen in fear, feeling rooted to the spot in shock, thinking, *I want to go home.*

Brad, on the other hand, was thinking, *why would the military drop a camouflage box with a person in it in the middle of the desert?* He figured they were using the ship as a landmark. But again, why?

Chapter 4

Brad thought for a minute and said, "Hey, they didn't take the box. I'm going to go back down there and take some pictures. Angela, you stay here with Macks."

"Don't go. What if they come back?" Angela was white with fear. "Something is wrong here. I can feel it."

"I'll be okay. If I see 'em, I'll hide. There's plenty of sagebrush down there." They argued for a few minutes. Nevertheless, off he went before she could argue any more with him.

She thought, *If it's a stealth chopper, you won't hear it and you may not see it before it's too late.* Angela didn't like any of this and just wanted to get the heck out of there. She wanted to go home; this wasn't fun anymore.

Nevertheless, Angela and Macks hid in the bushes, and she watched him with the binoculars as Brad ran toward the box. Brad started taking pictures of the inside and outside of the box. He picked up something from inside the box and put it in his shirt pocket. Then he started taking more photos, this time of the outside of the ship. He climbed onto the vessel's deck and took pictures of the insides of the cabin. He stopped, looked around, jumped off the bridge of the ship and started hurrying back up the mountain.

"What's going on?" said Angela to herself. She hadn't heard or seen anything, *Why was he in such a hurry now?*

Brad got to their shelter, out of breath. "You're not gonna believe what I just saw!"

"What?"

"For one, the inside of the box was like a coffin, lined with foam. My guess is it was so the drop from the chopper would not hurt him, or *it,* whatever it was, that was inside. Secondly and worse yet, inside the ship's cabin, there were several weird remains of animals, *strange* animals. It looks like they crawled into the vessel, got stuck and died. What in the heck is going on here? I'll go back later to check it out and go inside the ship to see what the animals are all about."

Angela was scared. "No, honey, let's go back and get the authorities. You have pictures for proof, right? I'm worried about Macks and us." Her voice cracked with fear.

Brad thought for a moment. "Maybe you are right; we do need the authorities out here. We could go back halfway and see if we have cell service. Damn, I should have brought the satellite phone."

Angela looked at him. "What satellite phone?"

Sheepishly, he looked at her. "I will tell you about it later." He forgot that she didn't know he had bought one for the man cave.

She started to say something else, but was too scared to argue with him at this point. However, they would talk about it later. Nevertheless, they both simply sat there in the shelter, hesitant to move and not talking. Both were thinking over the situation. After a few minutes of sitting, Angela opened her backpack. She took out some peanut butter and jelly sandwiches, which they devoured, giving some to Macks. Whenever she was nervous or scared, she gets hungry. However, in this case, Brad was hungry too.

A good thirty minutes or more had gone by since all the activity had occurred. What in the heck had they seen? What had been in the box? It was human… or was it? Well, it moved, so it was alive, whatever it was.

Finally, Brad took the binoculars again and looked one more time at the ship... *What the?* The box was gone. Now he was alarmed and starting to sweat. They hadn't heard anyone or anything that was able to move that box, so where did it go? To move it would take two or three healthy men if they did not have any equipment. He didn't want to scare Angela, so he said nothing about the box, but he knew they needed to get the heck out of there.

He thought, *I guess we could wait until dark, but I hate traveling at night.* He had not brought night goggles, and it would be really dark out here. There was no moon, only stars. They could get hurt. What was he going to tell Angela? Brad was having problems thinking as he sat there sweating like a pig. *Breathe, Brad, breathe,* he said to himself.

Angela could sense something was terribly wrong by Brad's body language, but she was afraid to ask. Her mind was racing and she just wanted to run, but something told her that wasn't a smart thing to do. They were safe for now, and they both had survival training and guns. *They would be okay,* at least that was what she was telling herself. They had to ride out whatever was happening, as it was a good six hours fast walk back to the car. A lot could happen to them in that period of time. *The time...* she thought. With all that was going on, Angela had lost track of what time it was; nervously, she glanced at her watch. It was after five. An hour or so and it would be dark. *What were they going to do?*

Chapter 5

It was dusk. Nothing else had happened; the ship was still there, yet the box was definitely gone. Brad thought it best that they start moving, but his gut kept telling him to stay put, or maybe it was fear. *It is not fear. I am not afraid of anything*, he thought, but he always listened to his gut. Was someone or something out there waiting for them to show themselves? Hell, yes!

He figured that whoever was out there knew that he and Angela were around somewhere. Whatever it was that had been in the box must have told them. Angela fed Macks his supper and they sat in the shelter and waited. She never asked what he wanted to do, as she was content to stay put too. Finally, Angela laid out their sleeping bags so they would have some warmth. They would not be able to set up the tent tonight. The bushes were their tent. With little or no talking, they decided they would ride out the night in the bush shelter and leave in the morning.

The night was not as pleasant as the night before, except for the sweet smell of sage. They didn't have a fire or watch the stars and talk about their trip. Neither one of them were talking. They zipped the sleeping bags together and Macks got in the middle. There was no laughing or joking tonight. Hopefully, they would stay warm, and Macks would warn them if anyone or anything got close. This adventure was no longer fun; in fact, it was wearing on them.

The next morning was Monday. They were stiff from sleeping on the cold ground, yet they had slept well. Macks never growled or got excited during the night, so nothing came near to them. Brad looked through the binoculars to see if anything was going on in the valley, but saw nothing. All was quiet; in fact, *too quiet,* as they always said in the old movies. No animal sounds. No wild horses or any sign of coyotes… and still no box.

Macks stayed close to them as he peed; he didn't even want to run around. He also sensed things that were not right.

As they were getting ready to eat breakfast, they started hearing sounds. First a helicopter, then a motorized vehicle of some sort. *Are they back?* Brad looked through the binoculars; this time it was a little different. These vehicles also looked military, but this time he heard faint voices.

"Shit, what is going on?"

Brad looked down into the valley as a chopper flew over. He recognized this 'copter as a military stealth helicopter, too. However, this one was called a Comanche. He couldn't read the markings on the chopper. They stayed crouched as close to the earth as they could. Below in the valley, a military vehicle in the distance was coming to the ship. As it got closer, Brad thought about five or perhaps six soldiers were riding in the deuce and a half. Their voices carried up the hill. The men wore camo uniforms like the other men, and from this distance, they looked like Army too. Brad scratched his head and thought *what is this all about? Angela must be right; they are doing maneuvers out here.*

As soon as the vehicle stopped by the ship, the chopper took off. Several of the soldiers started to unload and began looking around the area.

They're definitely looking for something or someone, Brad thought. *Is it us they're looking for? However, if it's our guys, why would they be looking for us now? Because the person in the box told them about us. Why would they care? What in the hell did we stumble into?*

Brad was starting to sweat. He knew his PTSD was trying to take over. He was stressing and needed to get it under control. *Breathe. Take deep breaths and get control of yourself.* He felt for his gun and was going to put it on his hip, but his common sense and the look on Angela's face made him think better of it.

Brad thought, *Should I let them know I'm here and cut out this hide and seek game crap? Do I trust them...? Hell no, I don't trust* anyone, *let alone the government. But this is the Army...* With that, Brad told Macks to stay with Angela and for them to stay put just in case.

"Brad, please don't go," begged Angela.

"I'll be fine. I just want to see what's going on. I'm tired of hiding. They're Army, anyway, so they're the good guys," laughed Brad. He told Angela to have her gun ready. "You may not need it, but just in case." She thought, *Those words will be carved on your tombstone, Brad Benson: "Just in Case."*

She was on edge and not a happy camper; she wanted to leave the men below alone. However, Brad crawled over to the path, just to be safe. He stood up, brushed himself off and started walking toward the troops. Angela watched the goings-on through the binoculars.

Brad slowly walked down the hill as if he belonged there. Several more of the soldiers jumped out of the vehicle and fanned out around him with their guns pointed. Someone shouted for him to identify himself.

Brad shouted, "Brad Benson, Washoe Valley, Nevada."

Brad spotted a Sergeant, who waved at the soldiers as they lowered their guns. The Sergeant, a tall, older, burly guy, walked up to Brad and asked for ID. Brad gave the man his driver's license. The Sergeant hardly glanced at it as he gave it back to Brad. The Sergeant again waved at his men, and they relaxed. He asked, "What are you doing here, Mr. Benson?"

"I hiked in from Hawthorne to see this ship in the desert, the one over there. I have a permit to be here," replied Brad. He started to show the permit to the Sergeant, but he waved it away.

"Everything seems to be in order. How long have you been here?" asked the Sergeant.

"I started yesterday from Hawthorne and spent the night, a ways back by the creek. It's about an eight to ten-hour walk from the highway," stated Brad.

"See anything out of the ordinary out here?" queried the Sergeant as he started walking back toward his vehicle.

"Yes sir, I did. I saw a Blackhawk helicopter carrying a large box yesterday, and it flew this way." Brad didn't know why he was not telling the truth, but something didn't seem right. Also, there was something funny about the uniforms, now that he was close enough to see them. They weren't regular Army. Maybe they were BLM, but that did not make sense with this type of military equipment. He wondered who they were? A black ops group, maybe? If so, who did they work for?

The Sergeant turned and looked at Brad. "A large box, you say?"

"Yes, sir," replied Brad.

"I don't see any box around here, do you?" he stated as he walked back toward Brad.

"I am not sure if he dropped it, and if he *did* drop it, where, sir. You asked if I saw anything out of the ordinary. I figured a stealth chopper headed in this direction carrying a box was out of the ordinary. Could have been someone dropping drugs? I wasn't sure. Nevertheless, I was a good mile or so from the chopper. All I know it was headed in this direction. I tried to take a picture, but by the time I got my camera, it was gone."

"Too bad. I would have liked to have seen the photos. Why did you say you were here again?" questioned the Sergeant.

"To see the ship," said Brad.

"You hiked — by yourself — twenty miles or more, just to see this old beatup piece of crap?" the Sergeant asked.

"Yes, sir. My uncle practiced bombing it during World War II." Brad was not sure why he said that.

"Who else is with you?" snarled the Sergeant.

Brad thought for a moment and asked, "What's with all these questions? I have a permit."

"I'll ask the questions around here. Now answer my question. Who is with you?" the Sergeant growled.

Brad just looked at the Sergeant, stood firm, and said nothing.

"Arrest this man for trespassing on military land," he ordered his troops. Two soldiers came over and led Brad to the vehicle, where they tied him up.

"I have a permit to be here. I've done nothing wrong," said Brad. With that, a soldier took the butt of his rifle and knocked Brad out.

Angela observed it all. She stayed quiet, and so did Macks. *Oh, what am I going to do? Who are these people? They are definitely not Army.*

The Sergeant told the troops to fan out and look for anyone else. Angela and Macks lay still. Even Macks knew something was wrong; he didn't bark or growl, just laid still next to Angela. She knew if anyone tried to harm her, he would do his damnedest to protect her. Angela got her Glock out of her backpack, and they waited. She could hear the soldiers go by; one was really close, and she prayed he would not see or hear them. Angela was so afraid that her knees were shaking, and her heart was racing. She tried not to breathe; beads of sweat formed on her forehead. Macks twitched and wanted to get up, but she held him tight. A few minutes later, the soldiers came back by again, headed down the mountain. She heard one of them shout, "Nothing up here, Sarge." She swept her hand across her forehead to get rid of the sweat. She was safe for now. *But what about Brad?*

Brad was coming to, shaking his head to get himself back together. He didn't say a word. The Sergeant came over to him. "Untie him and let him go." A soldier untied him, and Brad stood up, a little dizzy. "Well, visit your ship, Mr. Benson, and stay the hell out of our way," shouted the Sergeant.

"Yes, sir." As Brad started walking, wobbly-kneed, towards the ship, Brad couldn't believe what was going on. He was boiling inside and beginning to sweat. *Breathe, Brad, take deep, deep breaths. Get control.* He wished he had his gun. He would have blown the bastards away, but he said nothing. He walked around the vessel, looking inside, but his mind was racing. He was so thankful that they hadn't found Angela. These guys were definitely not Army, but some

50

mercenary group, or something. He didn't know what. What in the hell is going on? *Breathe, damn it!*

The men got back into their vehicle and headed back the way they came, leaving Brad alone. As soon as they were out of sight, he ran up the mountain to Angela and Macks.

Chapter 6

Brad was being cautious, just in case they were watching him with binoculars. He crawled back to where Angela and Macks were. He gave her a big hug and patted Macks, thanking the dog for taking good care of Angela.

"I'm not sure what to do. Something isn't right, but I don't know what it is. We're safe for now. Let's eat something. I can't think on an empty stomach. We'll stay here for a while and see what else happens." Brad was rambling, as he reached into his backpack and pulled out some peanut butter and jelly sandwiches. It was their favorite food.

Angela never said a word, but simply sat there, frozen in time. They ate their sandwiches and drank water while feeding Macks a jerky treat. Finally, they started talking about what had happened while Brad kept watching the valley.

"I don't know why they tied me up, and then let me go. Nothing makes sense," remarked Brad.

"I want to go home, but I'm not sure it's safe to leave," said Angela.

Brad couldn't figure out what was going on. He did know he wanted to go through that ship and get a better look at those animals. When looking into the ship, just a bit ago, the animals did not look like they had been there for very long.

Brad said, "Angela, stay here with Macks. I'm going back down with the camera to see the ship one more time, going inside and taking pictures of those animals."

Once again she said, "I want to get the authorities and go home. I'm scared."

"I know you are, hon, but we'll be okay. You have your gun, right? And you have Macks." responded Brad.

"Yes, but, what if they come back?" Angela asked with fear in her voice.

"We'll be fine; we're hidden, and everything will be okay. You can watch out for me. You have the binoculars. If you see something, shout."

Angela looked at him; it was no good to argue. Brad had no fear of anything when he made up his mind. Brad's mind was racing; he thought, *I'm counting on them coming back.* He took his gun with him this time. Brad crawled back to the path and very casually started walking down the mountain again. He felt they were watching him, or something worse.

Brad went inside the ship. Whoa! He braced himself against the stench of the dead animals. He hadn't really noticed the smell before. The smell with the heat of the day in a confined space was overwhelming. The animals, however, had not been there too long, maybe a week, as they still had maggots on them. Brad started taking pictures of the animals. Something wasn't right. These animals were not what they appeared to be. It looked like someone had designed them to look weird. *What the hell? Am I going nuts? Is this my PTSD? I feel like I am losing control.* Brad was sweating profusely. *Breathe…*

The cement ship was old and damaged. You could tell it was built many years ago and they didn't build the ship for comfort. *Hell, no. It was made to be bombed, not sail the seven seas,* he laughed to himself. The ship had seen its glory days; there was crumbling cement from the bombings and the weather. He cautiously walked around the ship, looking for souvenirs to see if there were any. He thought maybe he would get lucky and find some old ammo casings. However, if there were any, they were long gone from all the other hikers that had visited the vessel before him. He took a lot of pictures. There were markings on the walls, but he didn't know if they were real, or planted like the animals.

He was sorry Angela did not get to see this after they had walked so far, but she would get to see the pictures. Brad didn't think it was safe to bring her down to the ship. At this point, if they were watching him, they would still think he was the only person out here.

A movement caught his eye, and he reached for his gun, *Shit, it's a rattlesnake*. He carefully backed away from it. He had seen enough anyway, and he needed fresh air. He climbed out of the cabin onto the deck. He stood on the bridge and tried to imagine his Uncle Jim bombing the ship... He could see the plane coming in and dropping its bombs. Damn, he wished he could have been there, or better yet, flying a plane and dropping bombs himself. Brad so wished his Uncle Jim were still alive. What a tale Brad had to tell him! He would have loved to have fought in a battle like World War II, where at least you knew who the enemy was. In Iraq, you did not know who the enemy was, it could be a man, a woman or a child, friend or foe, and they blended in with the crowd.

Angela watched everything with the binoculars, thinking, *I want to go home. Hurry up and get your darn pictures and let's get the heck out of here.* All was quiet. For some reason, she was extremely tense. She felt like Brad had been feeling: something wasn't right.

Even Macks was restless. Macks stayed close to Angela; he didn't like it here either.

Finally, Brad came down from the ship and started walking slowly back up the mountain. There was a huge *whoosh...* and a rocket hit the earth about thirty feet in front of him. The blast threw decomposed granite up in the air and into his face. The Comanche was back. *Damn, did it have to be a stealth chopper?* thought Brad. He hadn't heard it, or, shit, even *seen* it. The chopper was behind him. He started running in a zigzag pattern up the mountain. *Whoosh...!* Another rocket came about fifteen feet behind him as the helicopter flew over him. Brad was thankful that the Comanche hadn't fired its 20mm Vulcan gun at him with its explosive rounds. If it had, he'd be dead by now.

Brad was halfway up the hill, running at full bore. The chopper was swinging around and coming back at him again. "Shit!" he shouted as he ran and jumped into the shelter. Quiet. They all lay still. The chopper circled over the area, looking for him. Then it hovered almost on top of them, searching. Brad was afraid it would see them. The damn chopper could have body heat sensors. He covered Angela and Macks with his body, just in case.

The chopper was now hovering right over them. "Christ, he *does* have heat sensors." Brad kept his body covering Angela and Macks. He was not sure what he could do. His 9mm pistol wouldn't take down a helicopter. With everything that was going on, they didn't see the Blackhawk coming, the one they had seen yesterday. It came in perpendicular to the Comanche and started firing at the other chopper with its miniguns. The Comanche swung around in the direction of the Blackhawk and started shooting back. The sound of the choppers shooting at each other was like thunder overhead, and they weren't sure if it was safe to watch, but they had nowhere to run. Finally, Brad had to look. Then they both watched the sky. The pilot of the Comanche must have been by himself or else was a poor shot. It had guns and a rocket launcher. The Blackhawk, it seemed, only had guns. However, they both could maneuver quickly as they were all over the desert valley. The pilot in the Blackhawk was damn good. He zigged and zagged over the wilderness and was climbing in altitude until he was above the Comanche; then he started shooting. *Crap, this is a real air fight,* thought Brad.

Brad hoped no stray bullets would find them; again he covered Angela and Macks. Between both choppers, they had enough firepower to blow the hell out of the area and kill the three of them without ever noticing them. Thank goodness, the fight lasted only a minute or two, but it seemed like forever to Angela. Finally, the Comanche flew off, then the Blackhawk, each in a different direction. Both aircraft were a little worse for wear, but they survived.

"What in the hell was that all about?" asked Brad, sweating like mad. "This is crazy."

Angela was shaking and angry. Macks was growling. "I'm going back. I've had enough of this. We're going to be killed… for *what?* To see a stupid ship in the desert that your Uncle Jim bombed," growled Angela. As she started to get up, Brad grabbed her and kept her down. "Stay still! It's not over. We'll be okay; trust me," he whispered in her ear as he held her close. She was shaking like a leaf. "Let me go… enough of this crap, I want to go back. What about Macks?" she cried angrily.

Finally, Brad gave her a gentle shake. "Get ahold of yourself. We'll be fine." However, he didn't believe it himself. She started to calm down. Having been in Iraq, Brad was used to being shot at — if you can ever get used to it. However, this was all new to Angela. He held her tight as she cried uncontrollably. Surprisingly, he was in control of his emotions even though he was sweating like mad. He had to be calm, because he couldn't let anything happen to them as he had his flight.

The world was quiet as they lay there for a while; Brad, Angela, and Macks, all in disbelief. An eternity seemed to go by, but in reality, it was only minutes. Brad let go of Angela and asked, "Are you okay now?" She nodded. Brad said, "I want to check things out," taking the binoculars and scanning the valley. He could see nothing. He thought, *Why the helicopter battle? What happened to the box? What the hell is going on? I keep asking myself that. If the Comanche wanted me dead, they had their chance. Was this all to scare us? What in the hell is this all about?*

Whatever was in the box is the key. It definitely wasn't drugs. Something was alive in the box, as it had climbed out. Why were the animals not for real? Were they remains of many animals created to look like weird animals? Was that to scare people? Or alternatively, was it a prank done by someone else? Either way, he had some great pictures, and if they lived through this, it would be a great story over a beer or two. Brad laughed to himself as he knew Angela would not think any of this was funny.

Maybe Angela was right, and they should head back, but his gut kept telling him to say where he was, that it was not over. *But what is not over?*

"How much food and water do we have?" he asked

"We have four more sandwiches and eight bottles of water. Plus, some dry food and, of course, Macks' dog food," responded Angela.

Brad thought, *Okay, we can ride it out for another day.* However, he was not sure Angela could. Plus Macks needed to run, he was a sixty-pound lab-pit with pent-up energy, and he had been very quiet. As they sat there wondering what to do, they heard voices. *Shit, more people. Where are they, and more importantly,* who *are they?*

"Mr. Benson, please come out of your shelter with your wife and dog," urged a voice. Macks gave a little growl and jumped up. Brad quickly put the leash on him.

It seemed they had no choice. Brad and Angela came out of the shelter with Macks. They stood up, and there were four soldiers in camo ghillie suits. They had sagebrush intertwined into the burlap of the suits to blend in with the desert. They also had M4 automatic rifles.

"Yes, may I help you?" asked Brad. *What a dumb thing to say. How did they know my name?*

"I am Sergeant Jeff Lowe, United States Army, and these are my men, we're here to escort you folks back to your car."

"Why should we go with you? I have a permit to be here." *Again, dumb thing to say. I'm not sure if they're real Army; hell, I can't even tell any more.*

"We're aware you have a permit, however, we are rescinding the permit as you folks are not safe here. We don't want any civilians getting injured," replied the Sergeant.

Little late for that, Brad thought. However, Brad and Angela didn't argue with the Sergeant. He started to, but thought better of it. Shoot, they wanted to get the heck out of there anyway. They gathered up their belongings and started the walk back to their car with their escort. They walked about fifty yards and at the bottom of the knoll were vehicles... two military Jeeps. *Wow, a ride out! This was great. Apparently, these guys really are the Army.*

"Sergeant Lowe, I appreciate the ride and all, but... what the heck is going on?" inquired Brad.

"I wish I could tell you, Mr. Benson, but I cannot. However, what I can say is that it's highly classified, and you probably saw too much as it is," answered the Sergeant.

"I was in the Air Force Red Hats, and had top security clearance," replied Brad.

"Well, that was several years ago, and your security clearance is not any good anymore. Sorry, sir, I still can't tell you anything," explained the Sergeant.

As Brad climbed into the front of one of the Jeeps, he lamented, "We planned this vacation for over a year. All we wanted to do was visit the ship in the desert and sightsee. Well, we have seen the ship and I doubt that we'll ever come back," laughed Brad. "How did you know where we were?"

Angela and Macks climbed into the back seat of the Jeep. She never said a word.

"Your permit said you were hiking this weekend, and your GPS signal told us your location. I'm sorry your vacation was ruined. Bad timing for your trip," replied the Sergeant. He said nothing more about what was going on.

As they rode back to their car, Brad thought, *I didn't have the GPS signal on. Things just don't add up. What's with the two different Army types? Why had the choppers fought? What in the hell was in the box? When I get home, I am going to go over all the pictures I took on this trip with a fine toothed comb. I'll figure this out.*

Angela and Macks were just happy to be going home and better yet, they received a ride. This place was too crazy; she wanted the sanity of her home. She knew, however, that when they got home, Brad would need to go back to his counselor. The stress of this event was already showing on his face. She knew the signs. She knew his mind was racing and he was boiling inside. Hopefully, they would get over this incident without too many problems. Brad was strong. Home was going to look good after all that had happened to both of them.

Chapter 7

Home sweet home. Neither of them had ever been so glad to sit in their own chairs, in their own home, and relax. Macks was jubilant. He ran around the back yard running in through his doggie door and then back out again. Macks must have done that twenty times, releasing all his pent-up energy.

Brad opened an ice cold beer for himself and poured Angela a glass of wine. He gave Macks a jerky treat and told him what a great dog he was. Macks licked him and brushed by him for a back scratch. Macks loved to get his back scratched; he would jiggle his left leg as you scratched his back. Macks was happy to be home… hell, they all were. Angela was worn out. This happens to people who are scared; they fall apart after the stressful incident.

Brad thought, *Later, after we relax, we can have a good, hot shower to wash away the desert and order a pizza.* They were home, so that part of the adventure was over… or was it? Brad couldn't wait to check out those pictures.

On Tuesday morning, Brad got up very early and let Angela sleep. She hadn't moved all night. He wanted her to feel safe and be glad they were home. And after all, they were still on vacation, so she could sleep in.

It was hard to believe all this crap had happened in just a few days. He and Macks went out and got the morning paper, plopping it on his desk. Then he made a pot of coffee and took a cup down with him into his man cave.

He got his camera and took the SD card from his pants pocket. He had taken it out of the camera, just in case, when he was loading their gear back by the ship area. He had slipped it into his pants pocket, as he just didn't trust anyone. Brad put the SD card in his camera to see the pictures. He had some good shots, and they were still there; they hadn't been wiped. He loaded the card into his computer and saved the pictures to his hard drive. Then he saved them on a thumb drive and an external hard drive as well. He printed a set of the pictures as large as he could without losing the resolution, then grabbed a magnifying glass and started scanning the pictures.

He studied the photos of the animals. There were several: a rabbit, a deer and some kind of squirrel. Animals you would normally find in the desert. However, the deer had rabbit legs, the rabbit was a jackalope, and the squirrel had deer legs. They definitely had been mutilated. Brad felt this was a prank. Probably some teenagers from the Labor Day weekend who wanted to scare the people who hiked in to see the ship. The animals death was fairly recent, as they had smelled and had maggots, so that fit the time period of Labor Day weekend. He figured the animals had nothing to do with the box being dropped or anything else that happened. It was just an uncomfortable coincidence.

The box — or was it a coffin? He was pretty sure it was a box, as it was carrying something and it was alive. The box was what peaked his interest. The box had a weird indentation in the soft foam lining that was inside. It had to have been for a person, but not a very big one. Maybe a little over five feet tall and very slender.

Now Brad's mind was really racing. Something from area 51? A child? A... what? He tried to copy the outline of the foam from his pictures. Using a piece of onion skin paper he laid over the photos, he traced what the body looked like to him. Then Brad started doodling, making it look like an alien. He laughed at his imagination.

This box is the key; I know it. However, how do I find out what was in it? All of a sudden a light went on in his brain. Brad remembered he had picked up a trinket from the inside of the box; it was a coin of some kind. He ran to the laundry for his shirt and pulled the coin out of his pocket. It was dusty. Brad took a rag and cleaned it up. It was a coin from a casino in Reno: The Mapes Hotel. Things were really getting weird. The Mapes closed in the 80's, and this was 2016, meaning the coin was at least 35 years old.

Why would someone have this on them in a box dropped in the desert? After more wiping, he found the token was worth a half a dollar and had a date of 1967... making it 49 years old. He went back into his man cave and took a picture of the coin. It was in good shape, just dirty. A weird feeling came over him, and he knew he needed to hide the coin. Brad didn't know why, but he just felt a need to hide it. He taped the coin to the inside of a book cover and placed it on a bookshelf in his man cave.

About that time, Brad heard Angela upstairs, getting up. She was in the bathroom. He quickly picked up his mess and put everything in a manila envelope, taping it to the bottom of the drawer of a desk in his man cave. Brad did not want to upset her. He shut the door and bounced upstairs quickly. As he was sitting at his desk, he caught her scent, fleeting though it was. He was drinking from his coffee cup while reading the morning paper when she came from the bedroom.

"G'morning, hon, what are you doing?" she asked as she came over and gave him a kiss on the cheek.

"Oh, just sitting here reading the paper, babe. Did you get a good night's sleep?" He felt bad lying to her, but he just knew he should.

"Yep, I did after sleeping in the desert for two nights with one eye open and all the rest of the crap that occurred. Boy, that coffee sure smells good," she laughed as she grabbed a cup.

"Yep, it was an adventure. Well, we're home safe now, and we get to go back to work in a few days. Anything you want to do for fun with the rest of our time off?" asked Brad.

She thought for a moment. "We could take a ride to Lake Tahoe and have dinner up there."

"Sounds good. We could hike around Spooner Lake or take Macks to Sand Harbor."

"I don't feel like hiking. I think I've had enough hiking for a while, in fact, for quite a while," she smiled at him. "Let's go to Sand Harbor and eat at Incline Village."

"Okay, we can leave in a bit. You want any breakfast?"

"Not now. Yep, we can leave in a bit, but first I'm going to get a shower, wanna come along?" Angela walked back to the bedroom, smiling and drinking her coffee on the way.

Brad thought, do I tell her what I've found so far, which is nothing, really, or wait? *Let me think about it.* He didn't want her to think he was getting paranoid, but he was. Damn, I just don't trust anyone, but I *have* to trust Angela, she's my lifeline. He sank into his armchair to think and drink his coffee. Then it dawned on him what she'd said, and off he ran to the bathroom.

Chapter 8

A few hours later, they packed up the car with Macks and headed for Lake Tahoe. Before they left, even though there was nothing on or in his desk upstairs, he wanted to set a trap, just in case. He took a strand of Angela's hair from her hairbrush, wet it and then laid it across his desk drawer… he had seen this done in "Dr. No," a James Bond movie. He didn't know why he was being so cautious, but his gut was telling him things were still not right. On instinct, Brad locked up the house and turned on the security. He even left lights on in the house, figuring it would be dark when they got home.

They drove down Highway 28 to Sand Harbor on the way to the North Shore of Lake Tahoe. They had a great time walking around Sand Harbor; there were only a few people there, so he let Macks run and play in the lake. Brad would throw a stick, and Macks would go get it. Brad didn't throw the stick too far out, as the water in Lake Tahoe is quite cold. However, the Lake never freezes. After a few throws, he told Macks that they'd had enough and dried him off; he didn't want him to get sick. Macks gave him a sad look, but did as he was told. Macks loved water, cold or not.

They walked the shoreline to the rocks; Macks was checking everything out and peeing on the rest. He loved to run on the beach, maybe because the sand felt soft on his feet. They all started heading back to the car when Brad saw four new people on the beach. He put the leash back on Macks for safety reasons; not that Macks had ever bothered anyone, but just to be sure. People get all panicky about a lab-pit running loose.

They were almost to the car when Brad noticed that three of the four people were following them. They started walking a little more quickly, but so did the people.

When they got to the car, he told his wife, "Angela, get in the car, quickly," which she did. She was used to his paranoia.

He quickly put Macks in the back seat, removing his leash. He opened the driver's door and got in; the seat squeaked under his weight as he hopped in. The men were almost upon him. He quickly shut and locked the door, retrieving his gun from under the seat. Macks started growling as one of the men smiled as he approached the car window and knocked on it.

"Sir, could you give us a lift?" asked the man through the car window glass.

"Sorry, we're not going that way," said Brad. With that, Brad fired up the engine and began moving the car; they could hear the gravel crunching beneath the car's tires.

"How do you know which way we are going, asshole?" shouted the man as he again rapped on the car window.

The other men were now beating on the car and shouting obscenities. Brad held his gun up to the window and shouted, "Get the fuck out of our way!" The men backed off and gave him the finger as Brad sped off, throwing pea gravel up at them from the wheels spinning.

"All the times we've been walking or hiking, we've never had that happen…What in the heck is going on in this world?" asked Angela. She was scared and breathing hard. Her heartbeat was racing, nearly exploding. She just sat there, pale and quiet with her knees shaking and her hand on her chest as if she had chest pains.

"The scary part is I didn't know what they wanted. How did they get to the beach? Were they hitchhikers?" Brad wondered out loud.

By the time Angela spoke again, they were halfway to Incline Village. "I'm tired of being scared, and I'm never taking a damn vacation again," she said in a joking tone as her voice cracked. They both laughed as it broke the tension in the car.

Brad still wasn't talking, but he was thinking, *What in the heck was that all about...? What did they want?* He was worried and his stomach felt rock hard.

They went to dinner at the Incline Village's Hyatt Regency. There are many restaurants on the North Shore side of Lake Tahoe. However, while they were eating, he saw the same four men from the Sand Harbor incident come in and sit across the room. They were eating at the same restaurant. Was it possible that it was a coincidence? Yes. However, highly unlikely. In fact, Brad recognized one of them now that he got a better look. It was one of the army/mercenary guys from the deuce and a half by the ship. Apparently, at Sand Harbor, he had hung back. Brad knew without a doubt they had followed them, but why? His adrenaline was spiking. *We have to get the authorities involved. I'm no Jason Bourne or James Bond.*

The men were still eating when they left the dining room. They didn't seem to even try to follow, which worried Brad even more. Maybe it was his paranoia; maybe it's by chance they were eating at the same place. His rational mind said *no way.* Thank goodness, they had parked by other people, and there were lots of people wandering around. They got into their car, gave Macks a jerky treat and drove home. It did not look like anyone was following them. Brad thought, *when I get home, I'm securing the house.* If Angela saw the men, she didn't say anything, but he figured she had. She was white and sat silently all the way home. Their lovely day was ruined.

When they got home, Brad checked everything, and sure enough, the house had been broken into, as the hair was gone from the drawer. It didn't look like anything was missing. Maybe the hair fell off on its own. But his gut said, once again, *no way.* Thank goodness he had hidden the pictures and the coin in a safe place. Maybe that was what they were after — crap he didn't know. He'd check on them later to see if they were still there. *Sure they're still there. No one knows about your secret room... relax, Brad, breathe. You aren't even sure anyone was in the house. Go to your room and check the cameras' video.*

While Angela went to lie down, Brad went down to his man cave and rewound the video. Sure enough, three men had entered the house. He couldn't see everything they had done, but they were in his house, goddamn it! Brad started thinking back on his military training. *If I broke into a house and didn't take anything, what would I do? Plant a bug.* So he needed to look for a bug or a camera. He ran back upstairs and asked Angela to come into the bathroom. Brad ran water to muffle their conversation and told her what he thought was going on.

"Angela, while we were gone, someone entered the house, and I think they've planted a bug."

Angela thought, *Oh, god. Is he flipping out with all this tension? I have to stay calm.* "Why do you say that?"

Brad told her what he had done with the hair trick. She was aghast. *He really is flipping out. Stay calm and play along.* He also told her he saw three men on the security camera videotape.

"What security cameras? What videotape? What are you talking about?" questioned Angela.

"I will explain later about all that, but right now we need to find the bug," responded Brad.

So they both walked around the front room talking to each other about the incident at Sand Harbor, each looking for a camera or bug. Angela spotted something in the fan. *Shit, maybe he is right.* She pointed at it. Brad was pretty sure that it was a wireless camera that transmitted a video signal. The scary part is the receiver had to be fairly close by. The hidden camera might also have an audio capability. This hidden camera type has to be activated by remote control. Did they activate it when they came home? Someone close to the house has to be operating this device... but *who?* They had to be less than a hundred yards from the house. *Who are they?* and *That's too close for my comfort*, thought Brad.

Brad casually yawned and said,"I don't know about you, hon, but I've had enough excitement for the day." With that, he closed the blinds so the lights outside wouldn't shine in and when they turned the lights off in the front room, it was dark. The darkness would blind the camera. He put his arm around Angela, kissed her on the cheek and said, "Let's go to bed. It's been some kind of day. Hell, *several* days."

"Agreed," they said and hugged each other as they walked into the bedroom. Macks went bouncing along with them.

Brad had a pair of night goggles, four guns, and a large knife in the bedroom. He looked at the fan with his night goggles, and ever so tiny was a camera light and most likely it had audio too. He thought, *Do I take it down, get the authorities or what?* Tomorrow, they would definitely contact the authorities, but for now, everything had to seem as normal as possible. There was a real possibility that they, whoever they were, were currently watching the house.

Brad hoped that was the only camera and there wasn't one in the bedroom. He took extra pillows from the closet and added them to their regular pillows, making them look like they were in bed. Again, grabbing his night vision goggles, he held onto Angela's hand and Macks' collar and they quietly went down the basement steps to his man cave, hopefully unobserved by the hidden camera. He thumbed the door switch, and the door opened with a hiss and a thump. "We'll sleep in here tonight," he whispered.

Angela hadn't been in the room for months. When she walked in, her jaw dropped. "Oh, crap, Brad, what's been going on down here?" The air in the room smacked of different good smells, as Brad shut the door with a swoosh. Brad placed a special towel under the door. He had made this towel so that no light, sound, or odors came out of the room, and no one would be the wiser about his man cave.

"I didn't want to tell you... I know it is a lot, but see, it was needed," he said with a cocky smile.

"Brad, we need to see the counselor."

"I will after this is all over, I promise." He knew she was upset, and he understood. However, he had to protect both her and Macks, and this room was proving to be necessary. He couldn't let anything happen to them, not like his flight.

He showed her how everything worked. She was impressed with his thoroughness, but it was scary that he had done so much without her knowing about it. There was everything they needed, from food to a bed for Macks. Brad had painted the walls white to make it seem brighter in the room. He even put a mural of mountains on one wall. The room felt warm and comfortable. The lighting was pleasant; he had used blue fluorescent bulbs. A sink was attached to the wall with a water tank that used gravity flow. A compost toilet was closed off by a curtain in the corner. Everything you needed was there; even a coffee maker and stove using small propane bottles.

There was even a fridge with wine and beer. However, if they lost power, the fridge would revert to gas. He could use the inverter, but the fridge took a lot of power, so it was better to let it run off the propane tank. Brad had a fifty-gallon gas tank. When that tank went dry, if they were still down here in the room, they would just have to rough it without a fridge.

Brad had stored boxes of the small propane bottles in the exit tunnel, and he had another thirty-gallon propane tank as well. He also had twenty gallons of gas for the gas generator. He was prepared for the duration.

Angela loved her husband and trusted him more than anyone in the world, but this scared her. *Was he going off the deep end?* She just didn't know. While Brad was off doing something with the computer type cameras, she sat on the bed, ate chips and watched. She thought, *Will we get through this before he has a complete breakdown?* Macks jumped up beside her and helped her eat the chips. Then he laid down and watched too. He knew something was wrong; his people were upset. Brad replayed the tape for her, showing the three men upstairs.

"Brad, why would anyone break into our house? What do they want?" asked Angela.

"I don't know, but it must have something to do with what we saw at the ship," responded Brad. "I'm going to figure out how to make a bug sweeper and check the house."

"We need to call the authorities," said Angela with her voice quivering.

"We're safe here till I figure this out, and then I'll call the cops."

Angela didn't argue with him; he had his mind set, so she and Macks sat on the bed and watched, eating chips. Brad knew if there was one wireless bug in the house, there could be more. He did a Google search to see how to make a bug finder and found a YouTube video on the subject. As luck would have it, Brad had everything he needed to make the bug finder. He ticked off the list on a piece of paper: a 0.9-inch brass tube, a piece of 41-AWG copper wire, a toothpick, a wire stripper, some glue, his soldering iron and lead, and an RF voltmeter.

Brad put all of the equipment on the large table in the middle of the room. The instructions from the YouTube video were easy to follow. He stripped the insulation off the copper wire with the wire cutters. He turned the wire around the end of a toothpick 20 times. This created a coil. Then he glued one end of the coil to the toothpick and allowed the glue to dry so that the coil would not come loose.

He took the brass tube and ran the other end of the copper wire through it. He measured a half inch of wire from the end of the pipe. Next, he worked on the BNC connector. He inspected the stripped end of the copper wire, connected the first wire to the positive terminal of the BNC connector and the other wire to the negative terminal. Then he soldered the connections. He stuck the BNC connector to the brass tube with a bit of bonding glue. After applying a dollop of the glue on the outer side of the toothpick coil, he let it dry, then inserted it into the brass tube so that it was secure. To do this, he pushed the glued side of the coil to the side of the tube.

Next he took the RF Voltmeter and connected the BNC connector to the appropriate connector on the voltmeter, turned on the voltmeter and did a test. He had a burner cell phone, which he turned on and made a phone call. He placed the RF voltmeter nearby and saw an increase in signal, which verified it worked.

Now the detector was ready. He could simply walk around with the brass tube in his hand, watching for a change on the meter gauge comparable to what he saw when the cell phone was transmitting. That told him there might be an active bug in that area.

This brings us back to Tuesday evening...

Before he could go upstairs and check it out, Angela saw movement upstairs on the computer screen. "Brad, someone is upstairs," she said with fear in her voice.

Brad looked at the cameras as the floor in the front room creaked from people walking. Macks growled. The door to the room was shut. He quickly turned off the lights, and they sat in semi-darkness. The only light in the room came from the computers. There were three people with some kind of rifles walking around in the front room; Brad could not tell what kind of weapons they had, since it was dark. Brad and Angela watched them on the computer screen from the security cameras; thank goodness he had installed them. *How did they disconnect the house alarm system?* Brad thought as he called the

Washoe County Sheriff's office on his satellite phone and told them what was going on.

The people upstairs methodically went room to room. Their night goggles made it easy for them to see in the darkened house. When the invaders moved into the master bedroom, they fired their weapons into the heads of the figures on the bed with their suppressed rifles. There was no noise.

They walked over to the bed and ripped back the covers… and one of the men said, "Shit! These are *pillows*!" They started looking around, to see where Brad and Angela might have gone. One looked under the bed, another in the bathroom and the third in the closet. Then they heard the sirens. "Shit. Thought you cut the alarm!" shouted one of the men. With the cops coming, the men started pulling out of the house. The whole maneuver was completed in a military style, in and out fast.

Brad and Angela sat frozen looking at the screen. "What in the *hell* is going on?"

Chapter 9

Three Washoe County Deputies' patrol cars pulled up to the house as the black SUV was taking off, and two of the deputies gave pursuit. The third officer came to the house and knocked on the door, which was open, so he yelled in, "Is everyone okay?" Brad, Angela, and Macks left the man cave. Brad told Angela and Macks to get into the hideaway under the stairs and lock the door. Then he ran up the stairs, shouting, "We're okay, but they shot the dummies in our bed."

"What's going on? Is the house clear, Brad?" asked the deputy before he stepped into the front room.

"Yeah, they all left when you guys showed up," replied Brad as he turned on the lights in the house, remembering the camera.

Brad saw the deputy was Sgt. Rick Anderson; they knew each other. Rick and Brad had gone to school together, plus Rick had helped Brad out of a couple of fights he had gotten into when he was drinking. Rick knew Brad was working on controlling his PTSD as well. They had become good friends. They had even played football together, and had a winning season.

Brad gave him a firm handshake and said, "I'm really glad it's you that came out. Let's step outside for a minute." They went out on the front porch. Brad said, "We have a wireless camera, probably with audio, in the house, that has been planted by someone, not sure who… it's a long story." Brad pointed to where they suspected the camera was placed in the fan.

Sgt. Anderson called for a Crime Scene Investigation (CSI) crew and a bug sweeper. He thought, *I hope this is for real, and not just* *part of Brad's PTSD.* While they were talking, the other officers came driving back. "We lost them, but I got a partial plate. I've called it in and put out a BOLO* (be on the lookout) for them," said Officer Pat Nelson. "Good job," said Rick.

Brad and the officers went into the bedroom to see what damage had been done to the pillows. They found that the pillows hadn't been shot with bullets — they'd been shot with tranquilizer darts! Brad hit his forehead with his hand. "Shit!" Whoever was responsible, they weren't planning on killing them — they were going to *kidnap* them. What in the hell was going on?

Brad was sweating, and Rick observed his tension. Everyone in the room was uncomfortable; Rick adjusted his utility belt and wasn't sure what to do next. Maybe the CSI team would know what was going on. "Brad, tell me again everything you know about what happened here."

They went back outside, and Brad told him everything that he knew, with the exception that he didn't mention his secret room. He said that he, along with Angela and Macks, had hidden in the basement food cellar under the stairs, which is where Angela and Macks were right now. "Oh, shit," he said, "They're still locked in there." With that, Brad ran down the stairs with Officers Anderson and Nelson following and knocked on the hideaway door. "It's okay, hon, you can come out now."

Angela was ashen white; she had never been so scared as she came out of hiding. Macks followed, staying close and loving on her. Brad grabbed her and gave her a big hug, "Everything is going to be okay now, babe, the authorities are here. In fact, Rick is here."

Rick said, "Why don't you guys start from the beginning, and tell me again what's been going on; the whole story, while we wait for the CSI team?"

Again they went outside; Brad and Angela told him about the hiking trip, the incident at Tahoe and now this. Brad still didn't tell him about their secret room or the videotape. He trusted no one.

"Why did you go downstairs rather than getting out of the house, and how did you know the men were here?"

"Rick, you know about my trust issues. Before we went to Lake Tahoe, I did a James Bond trick and placed a hair on my desk. When we came home after the Tahoe incident, I saw it had been disturbed. I didn't know what to expect. Then we found what we thought was a camera, so I laid out the pillows to look like us, and we hid in the stairwell to the food cellar. I have cameras on the property and in the house and can observe them from my phone, plus I have guns. I wanted to see what would happen. I'd rather be safe than sorry, and we were on our home turf, which was to my advantage."

Rick was having trouble wrapping his head around this story. While they were standing on the porch talking, the CSI team showed up and started moving their equipment into the house. Rick walked over to the lead officer and told them that they thought there might be listening devices and a possible camera in the house. They waited outside as the CSI team did its thing.

About twenty minutes went by, and Crime Scene Lt. Quill came over with a wireless camera in his hand. "This is military grade equipment. What's going on?" Brad looked at the camera, and before he could ask, Quill said, "I've disarmed it."

"I need you to sweep the entire house to see if there are any more devices," requested Rick.

"Will do, Sergeant," with that, the Lieutenant went back inside the house.

Brad, Angela, and Macks went and sat in their car, trying to doze a little. It was around 3 AM, and Brad's mind was spinning. He couldn't go to sleep. *We must have seen something that is so highly classified that they want to bury us away for a while... what did we see that could be that important? Who or what was in that box?*

There was a knock on the window. It was Sgt. Anderson.

Brad rolled down his window and said, "Yeah, Rick, what did they find?"

"They found another bug on the phone; no more cameras. The needles shot into the pillows are bear tranquilizers, pretty easy to obtain. Other than that the house is clean and secured."

"I'm not sure what to do. Should we stay here or go somewhere else?"

"I suspect that if these guys want you, they'll try again. Where do you think you would be safest?" asked Rick.

"I don't know. They seem to know our every move," sighed Brad.

Rick gave him a funny look. "Give me your cell phones."

"Why?"

"Just give me your damn phones," he said, holding out his hand for the phones.

They handed them over. He took the cell phones and walked over to the CSI Lieutenant. They talked for a few minutes and then went over to the CSI team's van.

After a few minutes, Rick walked back to the car and said, "your phones had a tracker. We've disarmed them."

"Shit, how could they have done *that?* We've had our cells with us the whole time."

"Any good IT person could hack your phones, easy-peasy. I suggest you get burner cells, and that'll end the tracking."

Brad thought, *I have several burners, so that's easy enough.* "But that'll only be a temporary fix."

"Agreed. However, I'm gonna have my people do some research to see if I can find out what's going on. Again, what did you see going on by the ship?" Brad again told Rick every detail, even about the helicopter fight.

Finally, it was decided that they would stay at their home. Rick was taking their phones with him to have their IT people look at them. Maybe they could trace back the IP address of whoever bugged them. Rick said he would get back to them the next day to see how things were going, and he'd have an officer patrol the area.

Brad was pretty sure they were still being watched. He asked one of the CSI officers to drive off in their car just in case it had a tracker. They would leave the car in Reno at the Sheriff's impound lot. Brad had a motorcycle and the Durango in the garage, so they could pick up the car at a later time. He didn't think they had a tracker on those vehicles or the CSI people would have found it.

Brad didn't know how long it would take to clear up this mess, but he was going to get to the bottom of it. *I'm not sure why the mercenaries would even want us. Shit, we didn't see anything at the ship. We don't even know what the person... if that's what it was.., looked like. This whole thing is insane.*

After everyone had left, Brad, Angela, and Macks went back down to the man cave. They were safe in their home for now.

Chapter 10

The rest of that night was fine. They never left the safe room. They put a pad down for Macks to pee on, the poor guy, since they couldn't let him out. They loved on him and explained what was going on. Macks listened to every word and laid down beside them as if he understood.

Since Macks was being so good, Angela gave him a jerky treat. He ate that up in three seconds and looked at her for more. "That's it for the night, you little beggar," she told him with a smile. He gave her a big lick.

Brad replayed the camera's video to see if he could recognize any of the men. Angela was watching over his shoulder and said, "Isn't that one of the men from the Lake Tahoe incident?"

Brad enlarged the photo. "Good eye! Yes, it is." He was the one that had been pounding on the front of their car. "Okay, so now we know for sure that these are the men from the ship, the ones from the deuce and a half. What in the hell was it that we saw?"

They both simply looked at each other. Neither one knew what it was that the men wanted.

Brad searched a facial recognition site he had hacked into a while back. The man's face appeared. His name was Andrei Vyacheslau, a Russian educated and trained in America. He was listed as a mercenary soldier, basically a soldier-for-hire. He had a criminal rap sheet that went back decades.

Who did he work for now? Moreover, why did they want Brad and Angela? They now had even more questions.

After an hour of searching, Brad's eyes were burning, so around 5 AM both he and Angela crashed for a couple of hours of sleep.

Around 9 AM, Macks began growling, low and menacing, and woke Brad, who jumped up from the bed and checked the cameras. "Son of a bitch, here they are, back, and in broad daylight!" He called Rick to tell him. He could hear and see them upstairs; they were obviously looking for something. This time, they were tossing the place. Pulling all the books out of the shelves, pulling out drawers from Brad's desk, and throwing furniture cushions. Brad saw the police cars coming in without their sirens; their cars blocked in the black SUV, and then, quietly, the officers came into the house. Brad figured Rick must have left a few officers watching the place for them to make it back here so quickly.

"Hands up!" shouted the officers, their guns drawn.

The men were caught offguard and tried to get out of the house, but the exits were blocked by police. Seeing that they were surrounded, the men gave up. They disarmed and placed their hands over their heads, letting the officers cuff them. One of them said to the others, "It's all right, guys, we'll be out in an hour."

Rick showed up as the officers were placing the men in the back of the patrol cars and taking them away. He came into the house and shouted down to Brad, "Everything's under control; we have them. They're gone." Brad bounced up the stairs, thinking, *Maybe now we'll find out what's been going on.*

"I suspected they might have been watching the house, and they probably thought we left in the car, so staying here paid off," explained Brad.

Rick said, "And I don't even want to know where you were hiding." Brad shrugged his shoulders and never offered up any information.

He did tell Rick what he'd found out about one of the men. Rick took the picture and information with him when he left, telling Brad, "You will be hearing from me, I guarantee that. I just hope you've told me everything."

"I told you everything as I remember it." *Except about the secret room.*

Chapter 11

The rest of the morning was quiet. They must have drunk two pots of coffee to help them stay awake. Brad never left his computer. He and Angela tried to draw pictures of the men to the best of their recollection. He ran them through the facial recognition site, and another hit popped up. This one was an Iranian mercenary named Amir Shirazi. *Interesting... we have a Russian and an Iranian mercenary. Who hired them?* From the looks of the equipment, he felt it was the CIA, Homeland Security or someone like that. Apparently they wanted whomever or whatever the Army dropped in the desert. *Who or what is that?* Brad thought, *I had better figure this all out quickly before we get hurt.*

Later that day, Rick came by again to see how things were going. Brad told him what they had found out. He asked Rick if he had learned any more about the men.

"That's why I am stopping by; they were all released. We were never able to talk to them," Rick told him.

"What?" shouted Brad, loudly enough that Angela came running into the room. "Angela, they let them go."

"Oh, no. Why?" asked Angela with a worried look on her face. "I can't go through this again, Rick... Why?"

"The Sheriff got a call from a high-level Federal agency and was told to let them go or else he would lose all his federal funding for the department. They were heavy-handed with the Sheriff, and you know, he's an elected official and looks at things differently than us."

Looking at Brad's face, Rick quickly added, "I understand your frustration. I'm frustrated too."

"What Federal agency?" asked Brad, as he grabbed the morning newspaper from the table and threw it across the room. The paper separated and went flying everywhere.

"Sorry, I can't tell you. The Sheriff didn't tell me; he said I didn't need to know," lamented Rick.

"Come on, Rick, you know they're going to try and kidnap us again. Damn it, you *know* that! Or better yet, maybe this time they'll just kill us. They've already bugged our house and shot our pillows trying to kidnap us. Plus the one guy that we gave you the info on is *wanted,*" said Brad as he paced the front room, sweating. "What are we supposed to do? Hide forever?" He slammed a drawer of his desk. *Breathe, Brad —breathe!*

"I understand. What I *can* tell you is that you guys must have seen something on the ship you shouldn't have, or else they think you know something about the drop. It's one or both of those scenarios. I'll do my damndest to keep an officer around the area if you decide to stay here."

"We don't *know* anything... *damn!* And where would we go, anyway? This could last for weeks," said Brad, running his hand through his hair, pacing the room. He was trying to keep calm, but his anger was building. Angela came over and held him, trying to help him keep his cool. He took her hand and held it in his. *I've got to hold on to my sanity*, screamed Brad to himself.

"I'm sorry, Brad. The best I can do is have an officer patrol the area here, and all I can say is stay safe. Call me if anything happens," said Rick.

"That isn't reassuring," said Angela, "this is our home, and we are not safe in it." She started to cry. "I can't take any more of this!" Brad hugged her, but now he was getting angry again.

"Come on, Rick. You can tell me what's going on. I *know* you know," said Brad.

"I can't, Brad… I'm sorry."

Brad thought, *I can't count on anyone. Screw it, Angela and I will figure it out ourselves. We'll take care of ourselves. I will* not *share any more information; I'll take care of this problem myself… Angela and I. No one else can understand what I'm going through. Breathe, Brad!* as he pounded the wall.

After Rick had left, Brad locked up the house and pulled the blinds. He armed the security system so it would give an alarm if anyone tried to get into the house. Then he thought, *Shit, they got in before; security does not mean anything.* So he braced a chair under each doorknob that led outside.

They had three outside doors; the front room, the kitchen to the back porch and one to the garage. *Now you scumbags will just have to come through a window.* Then Brad and Angela went back downstairs to watch the security screen on the computer. They locked themselves in the secret room, knowing, at least, that they were safe there. They could stay down in this room until this situation is figured out. Hopefully, it wouldn't take forever.

Brad laid all the pictures out on the table. He and Angela reviewed them, looking for any clues, anything at all. He brought the coin out to see how it seemed to fit in all of this. They ran all kinds of scenarios through their minds.

There was one scenario that seemed to fit, but maybe it was too far out. What if the Army dropped a person whom they were hiding out and the other Federal agency was trying to find them? That agency appeared to be using hired mercenaries to get that person — but why? Brad wiped his brow and rubbed his head. *Shit… why the drop by the ship? Because it was a landmark? Where did they take the person, and…*

Just then, the house phone rang, and "PRIVATE NUMBER" came up on the caller ID. Neither of them answered. The answering machine came on, and a voice started talking. "Hey, Brad, this is Bryon. How are you? Haven't talked to you in a while. Give me a call at 775-555-2294."

Angela went to pick up the phone, but Brad grabbed her hand and shook his head no. "I haven't heard from him in almost a year — why now?"

"But… you guys are buddies, shoot, you're more than that," replied Angela, giving Brad a questioning look.

"Yeah, yeah, but I don't know what he's been doing over the past year. He could be part of this."

"Brad, that's your PTSD talking."

"Maybe… but I want to be sure."

They sat quietly, eating a nice meal of chili, beans and cornbread. Macks was happy; he got to eat and he had his bed, so everything was fine with him, except he was restless. They knew that they had to take him upstairs and let him run for a bit. Brad checked the cameras; everything looked clear, so he and Macks went up the stairs. Macks was so excited to run in the yard; he ran around like a madman, peeing on everything and then he went behind the bushes to do his duty.

Brad looked around and didn't see anybody, but he knew he was being watched. After about fifteen minutes, they went back into the house. He locked up the house and left a light on in the front room. Once again, he placed a chair under the doorknob on the back porch door. The other two doors still had their chair braces from earlier. He and Macks went back downstairs to the man cave. Macks was content; he was with his people.

Basically, it was like they *had* been kidnapped; they were stuck in their own house. Brad knew they were watching him, waiting for him to make a slip… but who *were* they? Well, if he had to be a captive in his own home, he would do research. Brad had so many questions about what was going on, and he had to find the answers. Why wouldn't Rick tell him what Federal Agency was involved? Why had Bryon called? *I have all these questions. Well, I'm going to try to find the answers. We can't live like this, and no one seems to care what could happen to us.*

Angela was watching Brad with a worried look on her face. *This situation is tearing him up. I'm so worried about him. I wish I knew what to do.* She thought of the sweat lodge, but that didn't feel safe right now either. She walked over to him and held him in her arms. "I love you and we're going to get through this."

Brad nearly burst into tears. *I don't know what I would do if I lost her.* He didn't say anything to her but that look was on his face, and she hugged him tighter. "I love you too, hon," whispered Brad. Macks came over and wanted his love, which they gave to him.

Chapter 12

When they went to bed that night, they slept securely, knowing they were in the man cave.

When they woke in the morning, they had made it to Friday. They had to return to work on Monday; *that* would be interesting. Brad thought, *I have to figure out what is going on before then.*

After checking his cameras, Brad found that everything looked okay. He took Macks outside to run and pee, which he did very happily. Brad still felt he was being watched. He caught a flicker of light from something up on the side of the mountain, like perhaps the scope on a rifle. Brad stepped back onto the porch and called, "Come on Macks, let's go in." Macks climbed the stairs with his head drooped, looking sad, and went back into the house. Inside, Brad gave him a big hug and a treat, and said, "Love you, boy," and Macks licked his face. Macks was tired of being cooped up, but he loved his master.

Brad fixed breakfast in the kitchen, constantly watching through the windows. Nothing. Not a good sign. He saw what he thought was an unmarked police car drive by, park at the big pulloff at the end of the street, and sit there, watching their house.

Brad made a pot of coffee and fried some eggs for them to have fried egg sandwiches. He looked out the window, and the car was still there. That was strange. Usually, they didn't stay that long. He was wondering if he should check on it when the phone rang. It was Bryon again. He let it go to the answering machine. Bryon talked for a few moments, then said, "Brad, it is most important that you call me." He ended the call by saying, "First There."

"Shit!" By the time Brad reached the phone, Bryon had hung up. *What is this all about?* However, Brad didn't really want to call Bryon back, so he didn't.

Brad called down to Angela, "Hon, breakfast." Angela came up, and they ate their breakfast at the kitchen table, giving some of their sandwiches to Macks. He thought he was in heaven.

After they had eaten, she said, "I see Bryon called again. You had better call him back. Something must be wrong." Brad was hesitant, for some reason, to call, but finally he did after Angela's prodding.

"Hi, bro. I saw you'd called. What's happening?" said Brad, trying to sound nonchalant. .

"Oh, I'm glad you called, man. A lot has been happening. I need to see you and talk to you," announced Bryon.

"Well, I have a little problem at the moment and can't really get away right now; can't we talk about whatever it is on the phone?" asked Brad.

"No, the phones could be bugged. I'll come to you. Where are you?"

"Home."

The phone was quiet for a moment, "Really? I figured you would be in a safe place," said Bryon.

"My home *is* safe... what the heck is the matter with you?" asked Brad.

"Nothing. Ah, okay. I'll be by in a bit to visit," Bryon said, and he hung up.

Brad said to Angela, "That was the weirdest phone call. I think his PTSD is worse than mine." He thought, *Why would Bryon think my house isn't safe, unless he knew something, or is part of this?* He looked out the window, and the unmarked car was gone.

He decided to call Rick and see what was going on. "Good morning, Rick. Wanted to thank you for sending the unmarked car to watch the house. He sat up here for a while, so I thought maybe something was going on."

"Brad, I didn't send an unmarked car or *any* patrol car out your way this morning. We've been shorthanded today due to a major wreck on I-80 and a few other things that are happening," said Rick.

Brad told him about the car and explained that that it had sat there for fifteen minutes or so. Rick said matter-of-factly, "Brad, you guys need to get out of the house and get to a safe place. I feel like something is about to happen. I will try and call Carson City Sheriff's Office for backup. "

"Rick, what's going on? I know you know more than you're telling me," insisted Brad.

"Just get out of the house quickly and get to a safe spot," Rick said, and hung up.

Brad sat there dumbfounded. *Do they have any idea what this kind of stress does to a person with PTSD?* He was ready to shoot anybody who entered his house, including Rick. No more mister nice guy. Brad was sweating, and his gut was rock hard. *What are we going to do? Breathe, dammit.*

"Angela, I need you to help me." He proceeded to tell her what was going on.

"Brad, we're safe here if we go into the secret room; let's ride it out. We have to find out what they want. Hell, even who they are! Let's concentrate on that." She talked as calmly as she could, but she didn't feel calm. She wanted to run as far away as she could. She was thinking, *What did we do to deserve all this crap?*

"Bryon may be coming to the house, and he sounded really weird. My world is crashing. I'm not sure how much longer I can keep the fear of hurting someone under control. Right now I want to punch a hole in the wall, but if I do I'll break my hand," Brad said, nervously laughing at himself.

Angela came over and held him again. "We'll make it, hon. This is what they want us to do… run and be afraid. Do you need some of your meds?"

"No, not yet." Brad thought, *I have to concentrate and screw my head on straight.* He thought of the tools his counselor had given to him to help him get through these times. *Meditate. Breathe. Take a long deep breath and go to your happy place.* He remembered how he felt in the sweat lodge… *ground yourself.* Finally, he calmed down and got control of himself. All three went back down to the secure room. He left the door open in case Bryon came by, so they could hear him. Brad checked all the cameras and everything looked normal; in fact, it was too perfect. *There were no birds.*

Shit, someone had put photographs in front of the deer camera, he was sure of it. Nothing moved on that camera, yet there was wind outside.

He checked the other cameras but didn't see anything… wait — was that movement? Hell, he couldn't tell any more; they were blind. The sweat started coming again. *Meditate... deep breaths. Think. If*

Rick didn't send that car, it had to have been them. God, who is them? *And they put pictures in front of the cameras while I was cooking breakfast, that's why the car was there so long.*

He called Rick, but there was no answer. He called Bryon as well, and got no answer there either. He closed the door and turned on the satellite radio to get news and turned on the police band. There was nothing new, just a story about a six-car wreck on Interstate 80. He left them both on, got up and opened the door, thought about it and closed the door to the room again.

Angela and Macks were sitting on the bed watching him. Angela thought, *He's really upset. He isn't sure what to do. He's not in control.*

Brad thought, *I can't let them down — they depend on me.* He felt something was coming down, but didn't know what. Now, just to be safe, Brad pulled out a couple of tear gas masks. He placed the special blanket under the door. Brad felt they were safe now, and ready for anything.

Something came over the police radio; a woman was calling the Sheriff's office about three men hiding in her back yard over on Marigold Street. That was only a quarter of a mile from the house. So now he knew where there were, at least three of them. Since he couldn't reach Rick, he placed a call to the Carson City Sheriff's Office and asked to talk to the Undersheriff. He had known Don Brown for years; they also had played football together in high school.

"Good morning, this is Undersheriff Brown, can I help you?"

"Don, this Brad Benson. Did Anderson get hold of you?" Brad asked.

"No, I haven't talked to him in ages. Why? What's up?" asked Don.

"I have a problem here in Washoe Valley, and the Washoe Sheriff's Office is shorthanded due to the wreck on I-80. I think I need an officer."

Don thought for a moment; he knew about Brad's PTSD. Was he having a bad bout again? He asked, "Is Angela okay?"

"Yes, we're both fine right now. However, at least three men have been trying to harm us; they have broken into our house twice. They were arrested, but released; Rick wouldn't tell me why except that they worked for some Federal agency. My neighbor up the road called into the Sheriff's office to report three men in her yard. I know that it's them; they're coming again," said Brad, nearly out of breath.

"Calm down, Brad. Are you safe at this moment? "

"Yes, we're fine, and I have weapons. We have security cameras, but someone has placed pictures over the lenses, so we're blind," said Brad.

"Well, only use the weapons as a last resort. Let me check this out and get an okay to come into Washoe County. I'll call you if everything is okay," said Don very calmly.

"Thank you, Don. Thank you. If they break in again, I'll be forced to do whatever is necessary to protect us." Brad thought, *I'm tired of this bullshit, if they come here again, I'm blowing them away...*

"Stay calm, Brad. Let me get clearance to come into Washoe and I'll get back to you," promised Don.

Brad sat there for a moment after he hung up. *I am getting the runaround. They think I'm nuts. Am I?* He looked at Angela; she was pale. "Honey... is it me? Is it the PTSD? I know I have a reputation with the cops, but that was over a year ago. I'm not sure anyone believes me," said Brad with a catch in his throat.

"I honestly don't know if it's your PTSD or not. I don't think so. I do know some men came into our house, not once, but *twice,* and it's upsetting to all of us. Damn it, I wish we'd never gone on that hike to see that stupid ship," quivered Angela with a break in her voice.

"That's it!" He jumped up and started going through the pictures again. *The answer has to be here.* He looked over each photograph with a magnifier. *What are we missing?* He said to Angela, "Let's write down what we remember of the trip." He threw her a notepad. They started writing down everything that they remembered. After they had finished, they compared the notes to the pictures they had taken along the way and at the ship.

Chapter 13

Brad and Angela were brainstorming. *Before we got to the vessel, a Blackhawk flew over, checked out the area, then came back with a box with someone in it. A Stryker came by and picked up the person. Why a Stryker? The box disappeared... how? A duece and a half came by with troops — not U.S. Military — wanting to know what we had seen, and these are the same people now trying to get us... Why? So they're hired mercenaries... by whom? A Federal agency... what agency? The Blackhawk and Comanche had an air fight. The Army showed up and escorted us back to the car; how did they know we were there? How did they find them? Weird animals on the ship. The 49-year-old coin.* Even with all the information written down, nothing made sense.

They had been through this before. What if the Army, in the Blackhawk, dropped someone that needed to be hidden, and the mercenaries who work for this secret Federal agency want that individual. Okay, but why are they trying to kidnap us? A light went off in Brad's brain. *Because I have the coin! That's what they want. How stupid have I been... that's what they wanted all along!* He felt so stupid. The coin meant something to someone. Brad retrieved the coin from the book and placed it under the magnifier. Both he and Angela looked it over closely. It was old and still dirty. It had little black spots filling in the letters on the coin. Weird.

Angela said excitedly, "I know what those are! They're microfiche dots. We use them to store records at the office. We have a reader at work. It's old school, most people use flash drives or external hard drives these days, but the boss likes this method."

"Well, that won't help us down here. We don't have one of 'them readers,'" he laughed.

Angela smiled, too, and laughed, for the first time in a couple of days. "True. And seeing as how we aren't the James Bond types with a closet full of cool spy toys, we'll have to use everyday stuff. Did you know you can just use an ordinary microscope? And guess what? We do have one of those, because of my nursing classes. I borrowed one to study different bacteria for a test."

With that, Angela opened the door and ran upstairs to the guest bedroom; Macks went with her. Brad sat there dumbstruck. His wife had this completely under control. A few minutes later, she was back. She closed the door and put the blanket back in front of the door.

"Now let's see what we have here." She carefully removed one of the dots with a pair of tweezers and placed it under the microscope. She turned the magnifier up. "Wow, there's writing on it!"

Brad took a look. "Shit, this is highly classified information about the United States! No wonder they want this. The Army must be hiding a guy like Edward Snowden or something, and this rogue Federal agency wants this information. I imagine this information could be harmful to this administration and worth a lot of money in the wrong hands. Damn...damn! No wonder they're after us," said Brad, starting to sweat.

"But how would they know we've got the coin?" asked Angela.

"I am assuming that they are guessing, and not really sure. That was probably why they bugged the house to try to confirm it," said Brad.

"Call Rick and tell him what we found," said Angela, who was excited about their find.

"I'm not sure we can trust him. He wouldn't tell us the agency involved, and he never did call us back. Plus, he never sent any backup for us. I don't know what's going on there. I'm not sure who to trust anymore," said Brad, pacing the room.

"Well, we can't do this all alone," said Angela with her hands on her narrow hips.

Brad thought for a moment and said, "You're right, but I think I'm going to try. I'm going to contact Sgt. Lowe from the ship. We know he's Regular Army and should be a safe person to deal with. He might tell us what's going on."

Angela nodded her head in agreement. "It's worth a try. Whatever we do, I just want this mess over."

With that, Brad went on the computer and started researching Army personnel files. A while back he had hacked into them just to see if he could. After a few minutes of searching, he found Sergeant Jeff Lowe's name and a phone number. There were several Jeff Lowe's, but he was sure he had the right one, as his military address was Hawthorne, Nevada. He picked up a burner phone and called the number.

On the second ring, the call was answered, "Sergeant Lowe here, can I help you?"

"Sergeant Lowe, this is Brad Benson. We met by the ship in the desert, and you escorted us out," Brad said with a tone of confidence.

"Yes, I remember who you are, Mr. Benson. How did you get this number?" asked Lowe.

"That is not a concern at this time. As you know, we saw a box being dumped by the ship by a Blackhawk helicopter. Well, the men that were after whatever was in the box, have been trying to harm us. I've been informed that they work for some rogue Federal agency. They think we have something they want, and I think I have figured out what that might be. However, we need protection." Brad was sweating and pacing during the call.

Lowe hesitated before answering, and Brad knew he was putting him on speaker phone. "What makes you think we can help you?"

"Lets cut out the crap, okay? We have the microfiche dots, and you have the individual. I just want my family safe. If need be, I will give the damn microdots to the bad guys, just to get them off my back," growled Brad.

"Calm down, Mr. Benson. Let's talk this out. If you have the dots, what do they look like?" Lowe asked calmly.

"Shit, man, do you think I'm stupid? They're on a 1967 Mapes Hotel chip, worth a half dollar." Brad heard someone suck in air, so he now knew this was what everyone wanted.

"Okay, calm down. Where are you?" asked the Sergeant.

"At my home, and you already knew that, because you've been watching us." Brad did not know that for sure, but it was a good guess.

"Yes, we've been watching, trying to keep you safe. We didn't know if you had the coin or not," replied Lowe.

"Well, you've done a pretty shitty job of keeping us safe so far — no offense, sir. However, would you please do so now?" Brad said with a slightly mocking tone.

"We'll send someone right now," said Lowe.

"No, I want you personally. I will only deal with you, or else I give the coin to the bad guys," snapped Brad. He was getting stressed.

"Don't do that. It will take a couple of hours or so for me to get there," said the Sergeant.

"That's fine; we'll be here. We're not going anywhere. Tell your men to move in closer and keep a better eye on us," commanded Brad.

"Please keep the coin safe. It's quite valuable," said Lowe.

"Will do." Brad thought after they had hung up, *Hell, they don't care about us. They'd walk over our dead bodies to get to the coin.* Brad was furious. *Breathe, get through this. Come on, Brad, you can do it. Go to your happy place.* Finally, Brad got some control of himself.

After he got control and could think clearly again, Brad put the coin back in the envelope with the pictures and taped it back under the secret drawer in his desk. Angela was pacing the room the entire time Brad was on the phone; she was scared. In fact, she was tired of being scared. This crap had to end! Poor Macks didn't know what was going on; he could tell his family was upset, and that upset him. He followed Angela as she paced the room. Finally, she sat on the bed, grabbed some chips and Macks jumped up to be by her. He helped her eat the chips, putting his head on her lap.

Brad was not doing well either. He was sweating and trying hard to keep his anger under control as he paced. He threw a plastic cup across the room. Angela and Macks both jumped.

Angela said, "Hon, take a deep breath and relax the best you can. I can give you your medicine if you like."

"No. It numbs my brain, and I can't think. I'll take it later if I need to," he growls. *Why did I pick up that damned coin, none of this would be happening... but you know, it wouldn't have made any difference because they thought you might have it anyway.*

The police scanner went off; units had been dispatched to the house. The funny part was that Bryon never did show up. *Wonder what happened there, thought Brad.* Rick never called back. So many unanswered questions.

Brad left Angela down in the safe room, just in case. She locked the door and put the blanket down by the door on her side. She watched on the security monitors to see what was going on. He went upstairs about the time two Sheriff's cars from Carson City appeared. Undersheriff Don Brown stepped out of one of them and walked up to the house. Brad opened the door. "Thought you were going to call first," said Brad, "But I'm glad that you're here," and shook Don's hand.

"Figured this was faster," replied Don. "Everything okay?"

"Yeah, we're fine, just scared. I know you guys think this is just my paranoia, but it isn't," Brad started to explain.

"No, it isn't your PTSD. I talked to Rick. He said to tell you he was sorry for not calling me. They have been slammed with a six-car wreck — apparently involving the Governor's wife — and a double homicide. Looks like some gangs decided to have a turf war. He figured you would do okay with your training, and he knew you had a hiding place."

"They — whoever they are — as I told you, covered up my deer cameras, so we've been blind. However, I've been listening to the scanner. Come on in the house."

The Undersheriff turned to one of his officers and said, " Joe, check the area and see what you see."

They went on inside and Brad started making some coffee. "Do you know who this rogue Federal agency is?"

"Yes. However, I'm not allowed to tell you, Brad, according to the District Attorney, I'm sorry," said Don.

"This is bullshit, and I'm tired of it. Crap, everyone knows but us, and it's our asses that are on the line!" Brad started slamming things down. He got a couple of coffee mugs from the cupboard and opened the fridge, got the cream and slammed it shut. He was sweating like a pig.

The other officer came back in. "I checked the perimeter and didn't see anyone. However, I did remove these pictures from your deer cameras, so they should be working now," he said. He put the pictures on the table. "It's pretty clever what they did. The pictures look like the area the camera would pick up. These folks have done this before," said the officer.

"Thank you, Officer. I've made some coffee. So I take it Rick told you guys what has been going on?"

"Yep, we have the whole story," replied Don as he and the other officer grabbed a cup of coffee and sat down at the kitchen table. "What's been going on since we talked?"

"Nothing. It's been quiet. Eerily quiet.The main thing was the cameras, and I don't dare wander too far from the house." Brad didn't tell them what he and Angela had figured out. "These men have military training, and we seriously have no idea why they want us. All we saw was a drop and someone get out, we don't know who or why."

"The bad part is the Sheriff's department's hands are tied, with them controlling the federal money. It is quite a conundrum. Washoe had no choice but to let them go," said Don.

"I disagree!" shouted Brad. "It's all bullshit! The one guy had warrants on him, and they tried to kidnap us."

"I know it's frustrating, but we have to deal with crap like this all the time. We arrest the bad guys and the DA pleads them down and they are out in no time."

"Two hours?" snarled Brad.

"We could talk about this until we're blue in the face. What we have to do is keep you safe right now," said Don.

"Thanks. I know you're right, but we're tired of being scared and not knowing who we are fighting against or why," replied Brad.

"Not to change the subject, but where's Angela?" asked Don.

"Right here," they heard Angela say, and up the stairs she came with Macks. "I have to hide in the food cellar," said Angela with a disgusted look, "Because it isn't safe to live in my own house."

No one said anything. The officers simply drank their coffee. Angela went over and poured herself a cup and got a treat for Macks, then sat down at the kitchen table. Brad opened the back door to let Macks go outside, and he went running to pee and play.

Chapter 14

The officers were still there when Bryon finally arrived. Brad introduced him to Don and Officer Joe. He told the officers that Bryon and he had served together in Iraq.

Angela said, "Well, I have things to do. I have some laundry to wash and fold. Life may be chaotic, but the chores still need to be done." She laughed and she and Macks went back downstairs. Angela did start a load of wash, but then she went back into the man cave and locked the door. She could watch everything that was going on upstairs through the security cameras.

Brad had carried Bryon to safety when they had both been injured. Both men suffered from PTSD from the incident, though Bryon's was more severe than Brad's.

Brad still carried a bullet in his body that the doctors could not remove, but Bryon had lost a hand and leg in the fight. The VA was able to fit his missing hand and leg with prostheses, but it had to be difficult dealing with those losses.

Like Brad, Bryon got to drinking and getting into trouble. However, the difference was that Bryon refused to go to counseling. Brad tried several times to get him to go or to come to his sweat lodge, but the last time Brad had attempted to get him help, Bryon told him to mind his own business in a very unpleasant way. They damned near came to blows. They had not spoken since that incident, about a year ago, until today.

Bryon wanted to talk, but he didn't feel comfortable with the officers there. He tried to act cool, but Brad could see right through him. They were too much alike. All four men sat in the kitchen drinking coffee and talking about what was going on. Don still wouldn't tell Brad anything about this Federal agency.

Finally the Undersheriff said, "Well, for now, it looks like everything is under control, I'm going to go. However, I'll leave an officer outside to keep an eye on everything until the Washoe Sheriff's Office can get some of their personnel back here."

"Thanks, Don, and thank you, too, Joe, for removing the pictures. We've survived so far, so hopefully we'll be okay. Eventually, these people are bound to move on to someone else. I just wish I knew why they're bothering us." Even though Brad knew quite well why they wanted them.

Brad and Bryon watched the Undersheriff leave. The other officer went out to sit in his car with the door open and do his paperwork. Only after everyone left did Bryon turn to Brad. "Do you know what's going on?"

Brad poured both of them another cup of coffee and sat down across from Bryon. "I wish I did, Bryon, but I do not." Brad proceeded to tell him the story, as he trusted Bryon at least somewhat. They'd been through hell and back together, and they were like brothers. Brad brought Bryon up to speed on everything that had happened so far. Of course, as was his practice, he did not talk about the coin or the secret room.

"Well let me tell you what I know," replied Bryon. "There's an agency that's been spying on this administration. Not sure what they're called, but they hired us, retired soldiers from all over, to do their dirty work. I heard they were sending some people to bring you guys in. They asked if I wanted in on it, but I waved them off. Said

112

you were a friend and I wasn't getting involved. Anyway, they think you have something that they want."

"What? Pictures of a ship and a box?" laughed Brad.

Bryon ignored his comment and continued. "The person in the box was a whistleblower who worked for this rogue agency. She got away with some valuable information."

"What the hell? A *woman?*" Brad was amazed.

"Yes. Her name is Sara Green. She's an IT person hired by the rogue agency. Apparently a red-blooded American; after she'd stolen the information, she decided to turn it over to the administration, so the current administration is hiding her out to protect her life until they can put her in a witness protection program. Not sure exactly what happened, but somehow the stolen information she was going to give them got lost in the transition. "

"What information? And they seem to think *we* found it?" asked Brad.

"Yes, in fact, they *know* you have it," said Bryon.

"What? What are you saying?" Brad's mind was spinning. The only person he had told was Sergeant Lowe. What is going on? Brad was sweating... *Damn it! I don't trust anyone, let alone the government, and apparently anyone that works for the government.*

"Your house is bugged," Bryon continued.

"Yes, I knew that, but the CSI team got them all. They did a sweep after the shooting incident," responded Brad as he got up from the table, paced the room, then sat back down.

"Not all of them. They hear everything that's said in this house," said Bryon.

"Even *this* conversation?" Brad turned and looked at Bryon; he was edgy and sweating. "So they sent you to question me? You are working for them, too?" taunted Brad.

"Aw… sorry, Brad, but yes, I am." Bryon hung his head for a moment, then looked straight at Brad and said, "Now hand the coin over, so I don't have to hurt you or Angela." His voice was hard.

"Would you really hurt us? After all we've been through together?" Brad asked calmly. "I saved your life."

"Maybe, maybe not. But it was your fault we got shot up in the first place," he fired back at Brad. Brad turned ashen. He was hurt and was getting furious. He had an urge to punch Bryon. *Breathe, Brad… Breathe!*

"That's bullshit, and you know it. You would hurt us just to get a damn coin? For Christ's sake, put it where it's at. For once, man up and tell the truth," demanded Brad

"Hey, I'll kill you if necessary. That coin is worth a lot of money. I can retire to some Mexican village and live like a king," said Bryon.

"So you mean you'd hurt me for money? You son of a bitch. After all that we've been through. We are — *were* — brothers! "First There" to protect each other!" shouted Brad.

"Sorry, bro. But yes. Now hand it over." He got up from the table, pulled back his jacket and showed his holstered gun to Brad. Bryon was also sweating; it showed on his shirt.

Brad ran his hand through his hair; sweat was pouring out of him, and he was having trouble hanging on to his sanity. Both men were. He got up and paced the kitchen, grabbing hold of the counter.

He turned and again looked at Bryon. From the look on his face, he could see there could be no negotiations.

"What do you plan to do? What will you do with us if I give you the coin?" asked Brad.

"Whatever is needed. You know me," he said with a smirk, "I want the coin and a new life. So whatever it takes," growled Bryon.

"Yes, I do," Brad said. With that, he grabbed a knife from the butcher block on the counter and threw it at Bryon, ducking around the table as Bryon pulled his gun. The blade struck Bryon in the left shoulder and slowed him down a bit.

Brad ran to the bedroom, trying to get a pistol of his own. Bryon came staggering behind him and fired off a shot that missed Brad cleanly. Having heard the shot, the officer outside came running into the front room and then the kitchen with his gun drawn and was coming down the hall as Brad shot Bryon.

Brad had grabbed his gun from the bedroom and fired off a single shot, finding its mark. He hit Bryon in the thigh, and Bryon went down. The officer stood by Bryon and told both of Brad and Bryon to drop their guns. Bryon tried to get another shot off, but the officer shot the gun out of his good hand. Blood was everywhere; from Byron's thigh, which was bleeding profusely, and from his hand, which had been injured by the officer's bullet.

Out of nowhere, Angela and Macks appeared to see what was going on. Brad took his eyes off Bryon only for a moment to tell Angela to get back downstairs.

Suddenly, Bryon popped something into his mouth and instantly started spitting up blood and spittle, coughing and hacking as he turned quiet and pale.

"Shit, he took some kind of tablet," yelled Brad. He grabbed Bryon and reached into his mouth to get the capsule, but it was too late. Bryon was dead.

Damn, there were still so many unanswered questions. Brad was sweating profusely. He had lost control; Angela saw the signs, grabbed him and held him tight. Brad started crying. The officer got on his radio, asking for backup.

It seemed like forever, but at last there was Rick with two of his junior officers entering the kitchen. He had a worried look on his face. Brad was fine now; he had control of himself. The house had taken some damage, with bullet holes in the floor, and blood everywhere. Brad was upset that Bryon was dead. For what? Money and this damn coin... Shit, why did Bryon kill himself? Brad knew why. If the tables were turned, he would have done the same thing. Brad was blessed to have Angela, his line to sanity. There were a few times in his life he had thought of suicide, but then he remembered Angela. PTSD eats at a person's soul until they feel dead inside, and it gets old living with fear. *God bless, brother, rest in peace.* Brad thought, tears rolling down his cheeks.

Rick wasn't that understanding. "What in the hell happened here?" he demanded.

Brad told him what had happened from the beginning to the end with Bryon's death. As always, he omitted any mention of the secret room or the damned coin.

Chapter 15

The house suddenly was as crowded as a McDonald's on a Saturday afternoon, except none of them were kids. Brad was beside himself; he hated crowds! The coroner and cops were everywhere, inside and outside of his house. Sergeant Lowe and two military soldiers had arrived to see Brad.

Brad had finally gotten control of himself after Bryon's death and could again think straight, but god, he hated crowds. Angela was sitting next to him, holding him tight. They sat in the front room; Macks had laid his head on Brad's lap on the couch. Sergeant Lowe was sitting in the recliner with a soldier behind him. The coroner was picking up the body with a cop and one of the soldiers watching him. Rick was pacing the front room in front of all of them.

"Let's start from the top… once again, what the hell is going on? Do you know how much paperwork this is going to cause?" he grumbled.

"I'm sorry, Rick, but he was going to do me bodily injury, so I had no choice. And anyway, I didn't kill him; he did that himself," replied Brad with his head down.

"But Brad… you stuck him with a knife and *shot* him," yelled Rick. "I should *arrest* you."

"Yes, I *did* shoot him; arrest me if you want, but he threatened to harm both Angela and me. I had no choice; it was self-defense," shouted Brad right back.

Rick turned his attention to Sgt. Lowe. "And what is *your* involvement in this adventure, Sergeant Lowe?" snarled Rick. He was tired and stressed from everything going on under his command. He didn't have time for pleasantries.

"I do not have to answer that question, as it is classified why I am here, Sgt. Anderson." The two men glared at each other. He continued, "The reason I am here is between Brad and me."

Rick demanded, "Well, *someone* is going to tell me what in the hell is going on..."

Brad stood and paced the front room. He sneered, "From what I gathered from Bryon, apparently the Army is hiding a whistleblower from this rogue "no name" Federal agency. Everyone thinks we have something that was lost, and everyone wants it. If someone would tell me what *it* is, I would gladly give *it* to them." Brad was now gloating at Sergeant Lowe.

"But you do have it," growled Sergeant Lowe.

"I don't know what you are talking about. What is it that I have?" asked Brad.

Sergeant Lowe just glared at Brad. "You called me, telling me you have it. That's why I am here."

Brad simply put on an innocent expression as if to say, 'Who, *me?*'

He started to answer, but Rick, who was taking this all in, interjected, "I want to see some military identification from you, Sgt. Lowe."

"Go to hell!" he replied. And with that, he and his men headed for the door and started to leave. Rick let them leave without saying another word to the Sergeant. Brad could tell that Sgt. Lowe was pissed; he threw a dirty look at him as he passed and said, "We are not finished with this matter by any means." With that closing remark, the small coterie of soldiers stormed out the door.

"What in the heck is going on?" asked Angela. Both men merely looked at her and smiled.

Rick said, "Brad, for your information, I ran Sergeant Lowe a few minutes ago, and he is Regular Army. However, according to my sources, as of today, he tendered his resignation from the Army. Apparently, from the information I received, he was suspected of also working with this rogue Federal agency." Brad stared at Rick; he suspected he had made the mistake of telling the enemy that he had the coin. Based on what Bryon had implied, this confirmed it. *Shit.*

"Now do you want to tell me what's *really* going on?" demanded Rick.

Calmly, Brad said, "Rick, as you know, I don't trust anyone; it's part of my condition. I'm not sure I can even trust *you.* You wouldn't tell me about the Federal agency, and you lied about getting us backup."

Rick sat down and wiped his brow. "You're right, Brad, I didn't get you the backup you needed. But you know that all hell broke loose in the department today, what with the wrecks on I-80 involving the governor's wife, and all. Honestly, I just plain forgot. Now, about this Federal agency, I'll *never* be able to tell you the agency's name, because, frankly, I'd lose my badge, and with a family of three kids, I'm not going to get fired for *anyone,* not even a good friend in need."

"I respect that, but you have to respect what I want, too," said Brad as he paced the room. "I want people to trust and believe in me, as our asses are the ones online. You can see why I'm not sure who to trust."

They talked for a few more minutes; Brad never did tell Rick about the coin, but he knew Rick suspected he had something that the bad guys wanted. To make peace between them, it was decided that Brad would contact the General that was over Sergeant Lowe and see if could solve this problem. With that, the police got ready to leave.

Rick said, "I'm leaving one officer here with you in the house."

Brad decided to tell Rick about the secret room for the officer's safety, in case the men came back. However, he had second thoughts about it, since he didn't know the officer. "Rick, I think we'll be safe. Just leave us a radio and you won't need to leave an officer."

Rick looked at Brad and could tell he was uneasy about having an officer in his house. He said, "Okay for now, but we'll be patrolling the area. You know you aren't safe. They'll be back."

"I know, and I'll protect my family any way I have to. You can be sure of that. Besides, you won't be far away." Brad smiled at Rick.

"You're right. I have your back this time," said Rick. "This time if they're caught, we're not letting them go, no matter what the Sheriff says."

After everyone had left, Brad locked up the house, pulled the blinds, turned on the security and blocked the doors. He left the porch light on even though they had dusk to dawn lights all around the property. He also left a light on in the front room. Then they went down to the secret room when they felt the house was secure. They fed Macks, because (as usual) he was hungry. In fact, so were they. The three of them sat in the secret room, watching the cameras and eating peanut butter and jelly sandwiches. They talked about what had happened and what they should do next. Brad still didn't understand why Bryon did what he did.

"I can't believe I gave the information about the coin to Sgt. Lowe. Who would have thought he was part of the problem? I just don't know who to trust. And Bryon, he would have killed us if I hadn't shot him. Life sucks." Brad was sweating and visibly upset.

"Breathe, hon. It's not your fault. I thought Lowe was a good choice, too. We'll survive this; we're a good team." She smiled at him and walked over to give him a big hug. "I love you."

"I love you too."

They decided to stay where they were, since it was the safest place for them. They had everything they needed and could watch the outside world for any trouble.

The rest of the day was peaceful; maybe too much so. The quiet bothered Brad. They now knew most of the story and about the coin they had. The question now was who did they trust to give the coin to? That evening, Brad googled Sara Green, but didn't find much out about her there. Then he went into some of his hacking and social media sites and learned that she was a liberal but believed in her government. It said she worked for the Feds but never gave the agency's name… *Damn.*

Social media indicated she was 26, a computer genius and had no children. From her picture, it appeared that she was a short little skinny thing that wore glasses and had a pageboy haircut. In other words, she looked like a nerd. However, she did fit the outline in the foam in the box. Then he Googled Sgt. Lowe's superior on the hacked personnel site, and it stated it was a Gen. Louis Ryker.

Brad wanted to get in contact with him but just wasn't sure how they wanted to do it. He had told Rick that he would contact the

General tomorrow. Brad thought, *Can I trust this man? If he was Lowe's supervisor, he might be a crook too. Christ, who do we trust?*

On Saturday evening, Brad and Angela did the usual things; they watched TV and played Chicken Foot, which is a dominos game; it's more fun with a group, but it worked all right with just the two of them. Brad took Macks outside and stayed back on the porch, just in case, so no one could have a good shot at him. Everything was quiet.

Rick called to check on them; he really was a good friend. They were getting used to staying in the room and in their house. Macks was glad to be with his people. However, he missed running around. He just didn't understand why they were being locked in this room all the time.

On Sunday morning, Brad went upstairs and looked out the kitchen window while making some coffee. Angela and Macks were locked in the room. He saw the officer drive in and out, checking on everything. Brad was hoping this mess would be cleared up soon, since they needed to go back to work the next day. *I guess we can call in sick,* he thought. *So much to think about.*

He took two cups and the coffee pot down to the room. He knocked on the door, and Angela opened it, since his hands were full. After closing everything up, they enjoyed the coffee with some croissants and grape jelly. He had defrosted the croissants the night before.

After talking for a while, they decided that Angela would call General Ryker and invite him over to the house. Angela was better at sizing up people on the phone than Brad. Around 10 AM, Angela called him. When he answered, she said, "General Ryker, I'm calling about Sara Green. Could you come and meet with us, say, around 2 PM today?"

He didn't hesitate for a moment or ask who they were. "I live about an hour and a half away, so that would be great. In fact, let's make it 1:30."

Angela gave the General directions to their house, and the time was set. Now they would wait to see what happened.

Brad called Rick and told him what they had set up. Rick said he would be there as well. He added, "The patrols say everything is quiet."

Brad thought, *Well, everybody is showing up this afternoon, so we'll see if the fireworks start.*

Brad knew that the mysterious Federal Agency must not be sure whether they still had the coin any more, or if the police had it, so maybe that was why it was quiet. Based on that possibility, Brad felt it was still safe to take Macks outside. He and Macks left Angela locked in the room and ventured outside. Macks was so excited, he ran the yard like he was crazy. He'd been cooped up forever, or at least, that is what it seemed like to him.

After a few minutes of peeing on everything and doing his duty, he came back to Brad sadly and they went back inside. Brad secured the house and down to the room they went. Angela was sitting by the cameras watching them, and if she had seen anything, she would have called Brad on his cell, but nothing. Brad thought *This is the calm before the storm.*

They decided that when during the meeting with Rick and the General, Angela and Macks would stay in the safe room and watch what was going on on the security cameras. It was safer that way for them, just in case. If she felt there was something fishy about Ryker, she would call Brad on his cell. After the Sgt. Lowe episode, Brad wanted to keep them safe, just in case. His paranoia was racing.

At 1 PM, Rick and two officers showed up, and Brad had coffee on for them. Rick said he'd run Ryker, and he was legit and was still with the Army. Everyone was tense; you could feel it. No one was sure what was going to happen.

At 1:15, General Ryker and three soldiers showed up. Brad thought, *We're gonna have a full house again.* He hated a lot of people; it was upsetting to him. He kept telling himself to breathe. Brad met Ryker at the door and introduced himself and Rick. Ryker asked where Angela was, and Brad said she went shopping. They all went into the kitchen, grabbed a cup of coffee, and sat at the table. One soldier was posted outside as a guard.

"How do you folks know about Sara Green?" asked Ryker, getting right to the point.

"First of all, thanks for coming. We saw Sara being picked up by your men from the box by the ship in the desert down by Hawthorne," answered Brad, explaining everything in detail about the drop.

Ryker must have been a great poker player, because his facial features never changed, "I'm not sure I know what you are talking about," he stated.

"Well, if you don't know her, you probably don't know anything about the *coin,*" snapped Brad.

"I didn't say we didn't know *her,* just that we don't know anything about a box in the desert," he lied.

"Well, I'm sorry you had to come all this way, then. I thought you were the right person for me to talk to. I figured that you were the

CO of the Army base there. Maybe there's more than one General and I got the wrong one," said Brad, getting uptight. He'd enough of these cat-and-mouse games.

Ryker laughed and said, "No, you've got the right man."

"Then lets cut out all this bullshit and get down to brass tacks," Brad said.

"Agreed. You have something that is ours, I assume?" asked the General.

"Maybe. But we want to hear the whole story," demanded Brad.

"I'll tell you the story if you have the officers and my soldiers step outside," Ryker requested.

Rick waved his men outside as did the General, leaving just Rick, Brad, and the General. "I trust your house isn't bugged?"

"No, it's clean." In fact, Brad had swept it several times since the coroners and everyone else had left yesterday with the little device he had made. Brad did not, however, tell him about the security cameras.

"Sara Green was hired by a Federal agency that has since, let's say, 'gone rogue.' We were aware of them and fed them erroneous information. However, this time, they had gotten their hands on some accurate intel. Sara stole the information after she had seen how damaging it could be to our government. She placed the information on microfiche dots. The only thing she could find to put the information on was an old casino coin. Nevertheless, it did make it easier for her to smuggle the information out. She could have transferred the information digitally, but she was afraid their security would wipe it clean, so she went old school. Sara contacted us and said she would give us the information. In return, she wanted to be safe, because she knew they would kill her. So we placed her in the witness protection program, where she is now.

"However, somehow in transport, the coin was lost, and it's assumed that you found it. The coin contains highly classified information about this administration's plans to defeat a terrorist group. The rogue agency didn't want that to happen, so they hired military personnel, shit, call 'em what they are, *mercenaries,* to carry out their wishes, as you all well know. We suspected Sgt. Lowe was involved with the agency and had fed him some false intel. But we were never sure if he was involved, because he was smart. However, just this morning, Sgt. Lowe resigned from the Army. This sent up red flags. We were concerned he had learned something important about the coin and that was why he resigned. This information is worth a lot of money to the other side, and if he had gotten his hands on the coin, he would have lived quite well in another country. That's basically the whole story."

"Were Lowe and his men in the desert when the box was dropped?" asked Brad

"Yes. And when he found out the coin was missing, I believe they retrieved the box, and they tore it apart looking for it. They were not sure if it was lost in the desert or if you had picked it up. They knew there was someone out there, because Sara had told them. Lowe assumed it was you because of the hiking permit."

"Thank you, General, for your honesty. I do have the coin with the information on it, and we will give it to you."

"One more thing; I checked you out before I came here and knew you would make the right choice. You were an excellent soldier," said the General.

"Well, thank you, sir. But how did you know my name? You talked to my wife, and she didn't give a last name. What about the permit?" Brad's paranoia was rapidly kicking in.

"You filled out a permit to hike to the ship with your wife Angela and dog Macks; I see all of those, and so did Sergeant Lowe," said Ryker.

"Well, damn… if you saw all the permits, you knew we were out there hiking that day. You guys put us in danger!" Brad voiced was raised; he was pissed, his face was turning red, and he was pacing the room. *Goddam government. You can't trust them!*

"Yes, we did know you were hiking out there, but we didn't think you were that close to the ship. The chopper did look for you and didn't see anybody in the surrounding area, so he felt it was safe to make the drop."

Brad was still angry, but he felt a little better. He remembered the Blackhawk was looking for something or somebody. This all fit, and that was how Lowe knew about Angela and Macks. He excused himself to go get the coin. "Help yourself to more coffee if you like." With that, he went downstairs. Brad no sooner got into the safe room when he heard gunfire from outside. "Crap, what's going on?" He looked at the computer screen and saw at least five mercenaries approaching the house. He quickly ran upstairs and said, "Rick! Ryker! Come with me."

They all entered Brads secret room, and he shut the door and placed the blanket under the door, as always. Angela and Macks were sitting on the bed, watching the screens.

Rick looked at Brad and around the room with a look of bewilderment. Brad said, "I'll explain later."

"Yes, you *will,*" snapped Rick.

From the cameras, they could see the deputies and soldiers hiding behind the woodpile on the east end of the porch, along with a couple in the bushes. They could see that one soldier was down.

Rick got on the radio and asked for backup from the Reno police and the Washoe County Sheriff's Office as well as the Carson City Sheriff's Office. All hell was breaking loose outside. One of the mercenaries was shooting at the house with a handheld rocket launcher (RPG) on his shoulder. *Whoosh...* part of the west side of the porch was blown away. Thank goodness the officer had heard the rocket coming and jumped off the porch in time, taking refuge in the bushes. Sirens could be heard in the distance; the cavalry was coming.

Angela was deathly pale. She was scared, but she didn't say a thing. She and Macks sat on the bed, cuddling each other, watching the screens as the scene unfolded. She hoped they were safe in the room, but in reality, she knew they were. Brad had built a veritable fortress.

As they all watched the cameras, more police arrived, coming in behind the men who were shooting at the house. It sounded like a war was going on outside. *Whoosh...* a rocket blew up one of the sheriff's cars, and it went flying into the air. Thank goodness no one was in it. The officers had jumped out moments before.

More sirens; this time it was the fire trucks and ambulances. From the cameras, it looked like there were about five mercenaries, who were all well-trained military snipers. Then there were about fifteen to twenty police officers, who were also well trained; some were Special Weapons and Tactics (SWAT) members.

The police were trying to contain the mercenaries to the front of the property by boxing them in. There were cops and soldiers in both the front and back of the house, with the mercenaries in the middle, and more cops coming to cover the outside parameter. The police were trying to close the box. However, Brad saw that one of the mercenaries was attempting to sneak around the back of the house through the bushes to get into the house. Rick radioed one of the officers in the bushes by the porch. He instructed him to come into the house by the front door and blow the bastard away.

The officer came into the kitchen and fired a long burst of automatic fire through the back door. There was a scream from the other side of the door; the officer knew he had found his mark. However, rapid fire from an automatic rifle started coming back through the door, hitting the officer, who yelled out. They both kept firing back and forth; then the fire from outside ceased. From what Brad could see from the back yard camera, the mercenary fighter was down; it looked like he was gut shot. But the officer in the house was also down. It looked like he had been shot in the arm and leg, and Lord only knew where else.

Rick called the paramedic captain to tell him there was an officer down inside the house. Then Rick said, "Brad, let me out of this room so I can attend to my officer, please."

Brad told him, "It will take two of us. We'll go together to get him."

Both men left the room and ran up the stairs to pick up the injured officer, who was lying on the kitchen floor. Angela and Ryker watched everything from the room. Within minutes, they brought the wounded cop into the room and laid him on the bed. Brad shut the door. Angela, who had almost finished nursing school, started first aid on the officer to stop the bleeding. Brad really had thought of everything, as there was even an excellent medical kit in the room, even oxygen. Rick called the paramedic captain back and told him everything was under control, and he didn't need to send someone to the house.

The battle lasted about fifteen minutes, but it seemed like it went on for an eternity. The police got the men rounded up and handcuffed. No Federal agency was going to prevail in helping them out of this mess. One soldier and the police officer in the room plus two of the five mercenaries were the most severely injured. There were also a few officers with minor gunshot wounds or shrapnel cuts from the rockets. The paramedics were tending to everyone. Despite all that firepower, no one was killed. What was damaged the most was the house and property and the one sheriff's car.

Angela could have several fish ponds in the front yard if she liked with all the holes left by the rocket explosions. Their front and back porches were both destroyed, as well as half of the house's front siding. A kitchen door and a front room window were bullet-riddled. The inside of the house was a mess. It literally looked like a war zone. There was blood from the injured officer and splintered wood from the hardwood flooring, and bullet holes in everything. Angela looked around. If it wasn't so sad, it would have been comical. It looked like a drunken party gone wrong. The outside was the worst. However, everything was fixable and no one had died. Angela was heartbroken, though: this was her home.

Chapter 16

Brad and Rick got the wounded officer out of the safe room and got it locked up before other people started showing up in the house. Rick and the General agreed to keep Brad's secret; they understood his need for the secure room, and to be honest, they were grateful for its safety during the brief little war. The wounded officer wouldn't remember the room, due to his injuries. He was in and out of a slight coma.

Their house and property now were swarming with looky-loos, reporters, and more police. The place was as crowded as a Black Friday sale at WalMart. Brad was beside himself; as always, he hated crowds. He kept wiping his brow with all the sweat. The incident had hit the national news as well as social media. However, no one from the Sheriff's Office heard a peep from the rogue agency — the mercenaries were on their own.

Macks was the only happy soul, he was in his glory; all these people, and smells, and the new holes. He was running around peeing on everything and getting petted. Angela sat on what was left of her kitchen table and wept quiet tears. eating Ritz crackers, thinking, *God, I hope it's really over.*

It took hours for everything to be settled. Brad gave the General the coin. Ryker gave his report to the police and then he and his men got ready to leave.

"Thank you for the coin Brad. We're sorry about your home, but I'm glad everyone is okay," said the General. He added, "This will help keep America safe," referring to the coin. Brad felt that they really didn't give a damn about them or their house, as long as they got their damned coin. However, Angela felt the General, at least, seemed to be sincere.

Brad and Angela gave their report to the police about the whole incident, leaving out the part about Sara Green, the coin, and the man cave. Brad knew Rick wouldn't say anything about the coin, either; it was the best decision for our national defense. Rick said he wouldn't mention the secret room, either, Brad hoped that was true.

Rick told him, "The Sheriff's Department hasn't heard anything from that Federal agency, so it looks like the mercenaries are on their own. Whatever was on that coin must have been paramount. These mercenaries were paid enough to make it worth killing and dying for."

Brad replied, "The information on that coin was highly classified and worth a lot of money to the right people. If the mercenaries had gotten hold of it, they could have sold it for a small fortune."

Brad thought back to Bryon and silently wept once again. He'd saved Bryon's life for this. *Shit, life sucks!* He thought, *I lost my whole flight. I'm a failure.*

Angela came up quietly behind Brad and put her arms around him. "It'll be all right." She knew that wasn't so, at least not right away, as he would have to go back in for more counseling. This episode had set him back quite a ways, especially losing Bryon.

Chapter 17

Life was almost back to normal for the Bensons. After fighting with the insurance company for weeks, they lost in the end. Their homeowner's insurance would not cover the damages to the house; there was a clause in the policy excluding "Acts of War." Brad said that it *wasn't* a war, it was a *police action.* The insurance company didn't care; they said it was considered war damage. Normal people don't get their home shot up to the extent they did. They didn't care that the police was involved. Brad told them it wasn't a drunken party. However, the underwriters didn't care, and denied the claim.

So it was up to Brad and Angela to find the money to fix the house. Brad thought with a couple of friends, they could do most of the work themselves, so they simply needed to save up to buy the materials. The major things that needed to be done were to rebuild the porches, replace all the siding in the front of the house, replace the doors and one window. This would cost over $3000. So they would just have to save up to fix the house or get a loan, which they didn't want to do. Angela was adamant about that. The sad thing was that they had to do something quickly, as winter would be here soon.

The first thing they had to do was buy a new kitchen and front room door. They bought a steel door with a window; it had a built-in curtain inside it for the kitchen. Angela had picked it out; she said it would let light in and she could see out without having to open the door. The front door was steel as well, with windows on the top. The two doors put a sizeable dent in their pocketbook, costing about $600 together. Then they would need to buy two windows; they hadn't done that yet. Instead, they hung heavy-duty plastic over them, until they had the money. Angela wasn't happy about this as it ruined the view, but it would work for now. At least, it would keep the bugs out. They laughed about looking like hillbillies.

A trip to the thrift store netted them a decent kitchen table and six chairs for $125; "Such a deal!" laughed Angela. "We'll eat hot dogs until payday."

Angela had cleaned up the mess and the blood that was scattered all over the kitchen and front room. She patched the bullet holes in the walls and the hardwood floors with wood putty and repainted the kitchen and front room. Except for the bullet holes in the fridge, stove and dishwasher, you never would have known there was a gunfight in the house. The best news, believe it or not, was that everything still worked. This would give them more time to save money to replace them.

While Angela was working on the patching and painting of the rooms in the house, Brad had taken their little tractor and filled the holes in the front lawn. In the spring, the grass would grow back. They did keep one of the holes so Angela could make a pond in the spring and have goldfish. He repaired the picket fence, by filling the bullet holes with wood putty and repainting it. For now, they were somewhat ready for winter. They knew they still needed to repair some of the siding on the house before winter. That was their #1 priority.

Brad and Angela had been working on their place every spare minute, trying to get the house ready for winter. They were outside on

Saturday about a month after the shootout, replacing some of the insulation and patching the siding to keep the house warm and animals out. Brad knew that, no matter what, they would have to replace a couple of sheets of siding, which were $90 each. They were so badly shot up, they couldn't be patched. They could afford that. He would go to town in a bit, get the siding, and maybe run by In-N-Out Burger so they could get these patchwork repairs done today.

Tomorrow they would tear down what was left of the porches. Brad would build steps out of the old wood to use for now. It would suck, but they'd get by. They both knew any day the rains or snow could start, as it was almost the end of October.

As they were working on the insulation, they heard a racket coming down the road. Lo and behold, three trucks pulling trailers came driving into the yard hauling lumber, windows and siding. A bunch of cars were also following the trucks onto the property. People started yelling, waving and jumping out of the cars and the trucks, looking as though they were ready to work.

After the hellos and the hugs, the people dispersed to start the projects. Rick Anderson came over from one of the trucks and said, "We're here to rebuild your porches, front and back, and to replace your shot-up siding and windows."

Brad didn't know what to say. He stammered, "Thank you so much, but we didn't get any insurance money for the lumber, so we can't do the projects right now."

"Not a problem! Everything here was donated by a local lumber company after they heard about your situation. In fact, some of the workers came from the lumber yard to help."

"For real? Sweet. We appreciate that so much!" declared Brad. Even though he hated crowds, he was almost in tears, overwhelmed by all the kindness.

Brad and Angela were in shock. They couldn't believe that all these people — some he didn't even know — wanted to help them. A group of about fifteen men — some friends, some strangers, some soldiers, and some cops — started working on the porches and siding. Then a carload of women and kids came shortly after, bringing all kinds of food to feed everybody. It would be a great weekend. Macks had kids to play with and all sorts of people to pet him, he was in his glory. Angela fought back tears and started working with the women. Brad couldn't believe the help. He started pitching in to rebuild their front porch.

Around 4:00 PM, Brad brought out the barbecue, and they started cooking hamburgers and hotdogs. Angela and another woman brought the picnic table from the garage and put it in the front yard. They put all the food on the table. There was enough food to feed an army. They had completed the back porch and the siding on the house; it was an excellent day.

By late Sunday, everything was done and all the people were gone. All Brad and Angela had left to do was the painting of the porches and the siding, which they would try to do before the rains came. If not, they would finish it in the spring. The windows were in; no more plastic covering them. They had their view back.

Brad and Angela finished stacking their winter wood pile back onto their new porch. Angela went inside and got Brad a bottle of beer, which he drank as they stood there on the new porch looking over Washoe Valley. Both were thinking how they were so blessed to have good friends and a great life. They would never forget the ship in the desert; the good and the bad. Brad once again thought of his Uncle Jim, and said, "What a story we could have told him." Angela said with a smile, "I'm sure he knows."

As they were standing there hugging each other, she told Brad, "This time next year we'll have another person with us looking at our Valley." Brad looked at her in disbelief. She smiled, and he hugged her tightly. Macks came up and gave them both a lick. Macks loved his family; little did he know it was going to get bigger.

THE END

Jay Crowley lives in Jacks Valley, near the base of beautiful Lake Tahoe, Nevada. It's quite a versatile area, with ranching, mining, agriculture, and gaming. The Nevada setting provides a lot of opportunity for varied types of stories.

You may enjoy some of Jay's other work, including the novella THE CABIN IN THE MEADOW as well as the short stories "The Voice In The Wind" from OTHER REALMS; "The Vacation," from 13 BITES Vol. III; and "Pennies From Heaven," from I HEARD IT ON THE RADIO, as well as "Out Of Nowhere," from the upcoming PLAN 559 FROM OUTER SPACE Mk. II, all from Five59 Publishing.

Visit Jay's Amazon author page at `bit.ly/jay-crowley`

Made in the USA
Columbia, SC
25 June 2021

40638358R00083